Ann Jacobs

LORDS of Pleasure

Ellora's Cave
Romantica Publishing

What the critics are saying...

❧

HE CALLS HER JASMINE

"This was an enjoyable historical romance with an unusual twist. The attraction between the characters was immediate and hot." ~ *Sensual Romance*

"This is a fast paced romp in the days of damsels and knightsefun and enjoyable. It is a great light read." ~ *Just Erotic Reviews*"

"The sex…is hot." ~ *Mon-Boudoir Reviews*

A GIFT OF GOLD

"Ann Jacobs writes a scorching book that will turn up the temperature of every reader! […]The ending of this book is hot and surprising. I loved this book. I was sorry when I reached the last page." ~ *Ecataromance Reviews*

"A Gift of Gold is one of the hottest, most sensual works I've ever read. Readers looking for something more than a traditional couple will be very pleased by this unorthodox and mind-blowing story; I know I was!" ~ *Fallen Angels Review*

"This story is hotter than a firecracker. You will be in a perpetual state of arousal while reading this book." ~ *Coffee Time Romances*

"Known for her erotic tales of wickedness and lust, Ann Jacobs doesn't disappoint in A GIFT OF GOLD.…In less than seventy pages, Ms. Jacobs has created a fully fleshed out tale that will appeal to the lustier senses." ~ *RRTerotic Reviews*

An Ellora's Cave Romantica Publication

www.ellorascave.com

Lords of Pleasure

ISBN 9781419954764
ALL RIGHTS RESERVED.
He Calls Her Jasmine Copyright © 2003 Ann Jacobs
Gift of Gold Copyright © 2006 Ann Jacobs
Cover art by Syneca

This book printed in the U.S.A. by Jasmine-Jade Enterprises, LLC.

Trade paperback Publication June 2007

With the exception of quotes used in reviews, this book may not be reproduced or used in whole or in part by any means existing without written permission from the publisher, Ellora's Cave Publishing, Inc.® 1056 Home Avenue, Akron OH 44310-3502.

This book is a work of fiction and any resemblance to persons, living or dead, or places, events or locales is purely coincidental. The characters are productions of the authors' imagination and used fictitiously.

Content Advisory:

S – ENSUOUS
E – ROTIC
X – TREME

Ellora's Cave Publishing offers three levels of Romantica™ reading entertainment: S (S-ensuous), E (E-rotic), and X (X-treme).

The following material contains graphic sexual content meant for mature readers. This story has been rated E-rotic.

S-*ensuous* love scenes are explicit and leave nothing to the imagination.

E-*rotic* love scenes are explicit, leave nothing to the imagination, and are high in volume per the overall word count. E-rated titles might contain material that some readers find objectionable—in other words, almost anything goes, sexually. E-rated titles are the most graphic titles we carry in terms of both sexual language and descriptiveness in these works of literature.

X-*treme* titles differ from E-rated titles only in plot premise and storyline execution. Stories designated with the letter X tend to contain difficult or controversial subject matter not for the faint of heart.

Also by Ann Jacobs

☙

A Mutual Favor
Awakenings
Black Gold: Another Love
Black Gold: Dallas Heat
Black Gold: Firestorm
Black Gold: Forever Enslaved
Black Gold: Love Slave
Captured (*anthology*)
Colors of Love
Colors of Magic
d'Argent Honor 1: Vampire Justice
d'Argent Honor 2: Eternally His
d'Argent Honor 3: Eternal Surrender
d'Argent Honor 4: Eternal Victory
Dark Side of the Moon
Enchained (*anthology*)
Gates of Hell
Haunted
Lawyers in Love: Gettin' It On
Lawyers in Love 1: In His Own Defense
Lawyers in Love 2: Bittersweet Homecoming
Love Magic
Mystic Visions (*anthology*)
Out of Bounds
Storm Warnings (*anthology*)
Tip of the Iceberg
Wrong Place, Wrong Time?

About the Author

Ann Jacobs is a sucker for lusty Alpha heroes and happy endings, which makes Ellora's Cave an ideal publisher for her work. Romantica®, to her, is the perfect combination of sex, sensuality, deep emotional involvement and lifelong commitment — the elusive fantasy women often dream about but seldom achieve.

First published in 1996, Jacobs has sold over forty books and novellas, some of which have earned awards including the Passionate Plume (best novella, 2006), the Desert Rose (best hot and spicy romance, 2004) and More Than Magic (best erotic romance, 2004). She has been a double finalist in separate categories of the EPPIES and From the Heart RWA Chapter's contest. Three of her books have been translated and sold in several European countries.

A CPA and former hospital financial manager, Jacobs now writes full-time, with the help of Mr. Blue, the family cat who sometimes likes to perch on the back of her desk chair and lend his sage advice. He sometimes even contributes a few random letters when he decides he wants to try out the keyboard. She loves to hear from readers, and to put faces with names at signings and conventions.

Ann welcomes comments from readers. You can find her website and email address on her author bio page at www.ellorascave.com.

Tell Us What You Think

We appreciate hearing reader opinions about our books. You can email us at Comments@EllorasCave.com.

LORDS OF PLEASURE

ಬ

HE CALLS HER JASMINE

~13~

A GIFT OF GOLD

~103~

HE CALLS HER JASMINE
ಓ

Prologue

When she extended her arms, she could touch all four walls of the cloister cell meant to become her prison for life. Damn, but there was more room in the oubliettes where her sire tortured his prisoners. Joan of Summerfield stared at damp, dank stones that formed the impenetrable walls from which soon there would be no escape.

Joan wanted to be a bride, but of a lusty warrior, not Christ. Six months ago, the fierce warlord to whom she had been betrothed had died in battle. Her brother Will's mettle had been found wanting by the same fearsome knight who had slain her betrothed husband. Later, while Will lay near death in the great hall of Summerfield, their sire had promised her to the Church if God would but spare the life of his heir. 'Twas though she'd been naught to him but a gaming piece, expendable in the cause of saving her brother's life.

A fortnight later Will had still breathed. As though Joan meant no more to him than the pigs and sheep he sent each Michelmas as tribute to the holy sisters, her sire had packed her off to this dismal nunnery.

She wept for the loss of her fine garments and cursed the chafing from this robe of meanest unbleached woolen. Roughly-made rope sandals had rubbed blisters on feet accustomed to slippers of softest silk. While Joan languished on a rough-hewn stone shelf in this windowless cell with naught but a scratchy blanket to ward off the cold, she fantasized about her old bed and its down-filled mattress heaped with furs. Her stained-glass window with its jewel tones of red, purple, and blue. The fine tapestries that had brightened the solar's massive stone walls.

She dreamed of a handsome, powerful dark knight who'd come and spirit her away to his castle in the clouds where he'd worship her body and teach her all the carnal pleasures denied her in this dismal place. Of lying with him and exploring his massive chest, his hard-muscled belly and rock hard thighs...his swollen cock and the sac beneath it that held his seed.

Her mouth watered and her cunt dripped hot juices down her thigh at the thought of her fantasy lover fucking her there, feeding his mighty cock to her mouth and even her puckered rear passage, as she'd seen her sire and his knights do to the serving girls in dark corners of the castle. She was made to love a man, not some deity she could neither see nor touch nor taste.

A real man, not a fantasy dreamed up in her mind.

Christ's blood. They'd not make her promise poverty, chastity, or obedience. She would never kneel before the altar and meekly let them hack away her hair 'til naught was left but bloody stubble. Joan would not live out her life in this prison of piety, prayer and contemplation.

For Joan believed in prayer no more. Spending hours on her knees had done naught to deter her lord father from consigning her to this house of pious horrors.

She snatched off her veil and unwrapped the wimple to let her hip-length raven tresses flow free. They'd not cut off her crowning glory. Not while she breathed.

Defiant, she stood and lifted off the robe that was her only garment. The chilly air made her shiver and caused skin abraded by the rough wool to sting.

As she had seen her sire's men do to the serf girls at Summerfield, she pinched her nipples until they tingled and hardened. Longing began deep in her belly and settled between her thighs. She moved her hand to her hot, wet channel and with one finger she found the tiny kernel where those tantalizing sensations were strongest. Light strokes of her finger on the sensitive flesh hardened it and heated her blood, caused a throbbing in her cunt—the empty sheath she'd been given to accommodate a man.

'Twas made to fit a cock, hard, thick, and pulsing, like those she'd seen when she bathed her sire's highborn guests. Since the convent boasted no man save the elderly priest, Joan pictured the knight of her fantasies and pleasured herself as she planned her escape.

The pressure built in her cunt, sending waves of tingling sensation to her quivering thighs, her breasts, even to her fingers and toes when it finally burst. Her climax spread through her body, bringing blessed release and hardening Joan's resolve.

Somehow, some way, she would escape this pious hell. Death would be preferable to an existence devoid of all earthly pleasures.

Chapter One

"I can scarce believe you turned down an estate that rivals Harrow, brother." Giles deVere, Earl of Harrow, shook his head as though he thought Rolfe crazy.

Rolfe deVere pushed back his mail coif and wiped the sweat from his forehead. As he drank his fill from a leather wineskin, he glanced across verdant fields toward a mighty stone castle that sat high atop a hill. His elder brother had gained Harrow in thanks for valorous feats in battle for their king, along with an earldom and estates worth fifty knights' fees—and a bride of whose beauty and passion the bards all sang.

"I'm certain better opportunities will arise ere I'm too old to seize them." Rolfe paused, met Giles's amused gaze. "'Twould have taken more than the generous dowry Lord Eudo offered to entice me into his foul-tempered daughter's bed. I could have stomached her lack of comeliness, but her tongue—"

Giles laughed. "I wager she could find other uses for a sharp tongue than nagging, should you teach her properly."

"I'd fear for my manhood." Given the chance, the odious woman would probably have bitten off his cock.

"You have a point." Giles's expression turned sober. "I would give you Hedgewick, were it not entailed."

Rolfe nodded, for he believed Giles. But he wanted far more than the modest estate worth just three knights' fees, a finer keep than the moldering castle he held as his brother's vassal. "Speaking of Hedgewick, I should make haste to return there. The steward has not the wit to maintain order among the serfs when I absent myself too long."

Rolfe's absence, occasioned by forty days of service they'd given King Henry followed by a week-long sojourn at Lord Eudo's stronghold, had lasted quite long enough to result in chaos at Hedgewick. Rolfe imagined the hall was filthier than when he'd left it, and that its ill-trained servants had swilled his ale and befouled the hall while the lazy steward had turned a blind eye.

"Give Lady Brianna my greetings," he said, picturing Giles's comely wife. She'd have kept Giles's servants firmly in hand at Hedgewick. Arnaud, the giant eunuch who was Brianna's constant protector, would have put the fear of God into any who'd think to defy her orders.

"I will. If Brianna's time were not so near, I would accompany you to Hedgewick. I will send you word when my heir is born. My lady wishes you to stand godfather to him."

"Or her." Though Rolfe enjoyed tweaking Giles's temper, he reckoned the chance for the child to be female was close to none. After all, they were but the third and fourth of five sons their father had sired, and they had not a single sister.

'Twas why he and Giles had sought their fortunes as mercenaries when faced with the alternative: joining the monks at a cloister their great grandsire had founded for his own brothers on the deVere lands in Normandy. 'Twas also why Rolfe needed to find an heiress to gain the lands and title he coveted.

After Giles and his escort veered off the road and across the fields, Rolfe continued down the track, his own much smaller entourage at his heels. Anxious for what few comforts might await him at Hedgewick, he spurred his destrier. His helm and coif removed now that they rode on friendly ground, he enjoyed the warm summer wind that blew through his hair, its touch as beguiling as a lover's.

Rolfe gave his young warhorse his head, and soon he'd outpaced his escort. A pity Lord Eudo's daughter had pleased him not, for her dowry had been impressive.

What he sought now was a bath to rid him of the grime of travel, fine wine to wash down the swill from Hedgewick's kitchens, and a willing wench. Such would raise his spirits ere he began again to impose his will once more upon Hedgewick's recalcitrant serfs.

When he noticed the forbidding walls of St. Benedict's Convent rising beyond a dense cloak of forest, he calculated it would take another hour's hard riding ere he reached home.

Courtesy demanded he pay the prioress a visit as he passed by, but courtesy be damned. The cloistered nunnery chilled him to the bone, even though he had only gone as far inside as a dank cubicle built into the outer wall where an old nun had accepted the alms he'd brought from Hedgewick last Michaelmas.

He shuddered at the thought of passing his life within such a place, locked away from the world and all its pleasures. A place eerily similar to the gray stone monastery where he had been ensconced ere Giles had rescued him and taken him on Crusade as his squire.

Glancing to his back, Rolfe saw his men at arms still followed a short distance behind. The convent chapel's bell sounded, its tone mournful as though pleading for the lonely souls inside.

*****

Bells rang from somewhere far away, their dolorous tones muted through the blanket of trees along the road.

Familiar sounds, yet foreign. They reverberated in her throbbing head like a hammer and anvil, nearly drowning out the clatter of horsemen coming closer with each clatter of hooves against the track's hard-packed clay.

She sensed danger. Though each step on her blistered feet dug the rope straps of her rough hemp sandals more deeply into her tortured flesh, she stumbled along. Exhausted, bruised, damp from the hovering mist and chilled to the bone, she veered into a clearing in the forest and collapsed beneath a mighty rowan tree.

Mayhap the mist would obscure her from the band of brigands she had sighted. And the horsemen she'd heard approaching from the rear. It mattered not. She could go no farther.

Closing her eyes, she slept. When she woke she screamed, for a band of ragged outlaws surrounded her, their greasy hands tugging at her garments, pawing lewdly at her breasts and belly as they tore the cloth asunder.

One shoved a piece of her robe into her mouth. "Silence, sister," he spat out as he shoved her to the ground. "Hold 'er legs. You'll have yer turns swiving her when I am done."

Another man snatched the veil from her head. "Look at this one's hair. This be no nun. Must be a runaway wife. Right pretty she is."

When he belched, the stench of rancid fat, sour ale, and rotten teeth made her retch into her gag.

* * * * *

Sounds of trouble loomed ahead, as eloquent as the sharp piercing cry that initially penetrated the forest mist.

Rolfe raised his coif and donned his helmet. As he spurred his destrier forward, he snapped down the nasal.

Coarse jests and raucous laughter directed him to a tree-shaded clearing. Setting his mace to swinging, he veered off the track toward the source of the noise.

Brigands. Likely part of the band of wandering thieves and murderers he and Giles had thought they'd routed ere leaving to do King Henry's bidding on the Scots border. Their attention focused on the wench they were bent on ravishing, the outlaws paid no apparent heed to the pounding of his destrier's hooves.

With a vicious upswing, Rolfe caught one knave full in the face. Blood spurted. Rolfe swung again and two more men went down. The last one of the motley band tried to flee, but Rolfe threw his dagger true. The man fell ere he could reach the safety of the dense woods beyond the clearing.

Bloodlust still burning, Rolfe dismounted and drew his heavy broadsword. He'd dispatch any who yet lived, straight to hell.

His breath caught in his throat when he shoved aside the body of a dead assailant, knelt, and looked closely upon the naked woman the curs had been about to ravish. 'Twas no hag, but the most beautiful woman he'd ever seen. Raven hair, alabaster skin, full breasts tipped with nipples of deep rose and a nest of dark curls at the apex of her shapely thighs. Her soft lips invited his touch when he pulled the filthy rag from her mouth.

"Who are you, sweeting?" he asked first in his native Norman French, then haltingly in the guttural Saxon tongue of the English peasants when he noticed the shredded remnants of rough homespun that must have been her clothing.

She answered neither question, but her sooty eyelashes fluttered. The deep blue-green hue of her eyes reminded him of a stormy sea. A sea full of fear—but something more.

Rolfe removed his helm, hoping the sight of his face might allay her fears.

He must be Lucifer, she thought when she found the strength to open her eyes. The dark angel of temptation of whom the priests spouted dire warning to every maiden.

She took in his regular features, pleasing to the eye. A strong jaw shadowed with dark beard stubble drew her gaze to clean-smelling white teeth between lips so sensual-looking she longed to taste them. He had a nose both strong and noble.

When he pushed the mail coif back from his head, he revealed silky sable hair cut short in the style of a Norman knight. His thick, muscular neck and broad shoulders hinted he would prove a formidable foe. And the rich surcoat of black silk he wore over his chain mail suggested he possessed wealth and power.

Then she glimpsed his bloody mace and sword. A foul smell of blood and offal wafted on the breeze from the corpses her paladin had dragged off her.

She owed this knight her life.

He drew off one gauntlet, then stroked her cheek with the back of his hand. "Would you tell me your name?" he asked again.

A simple question. Yet when she searched her mind, she found no answer. "I know it not, my lord."

"From whence did you come?"

"I know not." Panic rose in her like bile, threatened to rob her of consciousness again.

"Then I shall call you Jasmine, for your beauty reminds me of the sweet-smelling flowers of that name that grow in the gardens of the infidel. Fear not, sweeting, I shall treat you with the kind of care one as comely as you deserves."

She moistened her dry lips with her tongue, fought down a wave of panic when she recognized the lust in his glittering obsidian gaze.

But then she recalled her captors and their intent to tear her asunder. Her fear allayed, she let out the breath she'd been holding. If she was to be ravaged, better the deed be done by this beautiful demon than by the foul-breathed rogues he'd sent to their just rewards.

"What do you intend, my lord?" she asked, her fear warring with a hot surge of desire that began low in her belly and sent wet, warm juices to smooth his way.

"To banish the terror from your lovely eyes. And to love you so well that memories of yon foul knaves will vanish from your mind. I will show you the boundless pleasures a man and woman may share."

As if mesmerized, he ran his callused fingers down her neck and caressed the upper curve of one breast before turning his attention to its aching, puckered tip. His eyes darkened further. Then he bent and suckled her bare nipple as though he were a babe.

A cool wind chilled her naked skin, made her shudder against his mouth and hand even as heat built within her, turned her cunt to molten fire. He raised his head, murmured an apology against her breast, and moved far enough away to lift his surcoat over his head.

"Cover yourself, Jasmine. I would not have you catch a chill. Besides, my men approach, and I would that the pleasure of looking upon you be mine alone."

Jasmine. The name struck no chord in her memory, yet his gentle touch as he slipped the fine silk garment over her naked skin lulled away the remnants of her fear, leaving anticipation in its wake.

Her fallen angel would protect her. She doubted not that he would take for himself that which he had prevented her attackers from seizing.

Nay, he would take more. He would steal her very soul. And she could barely wait for him to claim her. When he rose and extended his hand, she laid hers there and allowed him to lift her to her feet. His body radiated heat as he moved behind her when she began to shiver.

When he pulled her close, his hands warmed her belly. His hot breath ruffled her hair. Even the fine chain mail he wore drove the chill from her back with heat generated by his powerful body.

This was no wandering knight, she surmised from the way he ordered the other knight and the four men at arms who apparently made up his escort to scout ahead and ensure that no more brigands lurked along the track. This was a nobleman used to commanding men.

When they were alone again, he stood and helped her up. Raising the hem of his surcoat almost to her waist, he lifted her with little apparent effort and set her facing backward in the saddle astride his great black destrier. Self-conscious, she arranged the split surcoat to cover her naked legs, but her aching center lay open, vulnerable.

"Where go we, my lord?"

"To Hedgewick Keep. You will be safe there."

Safe? She pictured soft bedding and fur covers to keep out the cold. Tapestries and fragrant rushes on the floor. From whence came the memory she could not say, but it seduced her.

He seduced her, made her yearn to taste and touch every inch of his finely honed body. To take him inside her and fill the emptiness there.

When he swung into the saddle behind her and draped her legs over his thighs, she could think of nothing but the heat and strength of his rampant cock that pulsated against her core through the scant protection of his braies.

"Who are you, my lord?"

"Rolfe deVere. I will keep you from harm."

As he spoke, he urged the destrier forward. Their bodies ebbed and flowed with the beast's motion. When she glanced down, the sight of his mighty sword straining at the cloth that confined it took her breath away. She edged closer, seeking, needing, wanting—

"Nay, sweeting. I would fuck with you the first time in my bed. Later we may explore the possibilities of mating atop a warhorse. Lucifer is young and not yet fully trained. I'd not risk the possibility of him tossing us to the hard ground." When Rolfe reached down and loosened his braies, his huge, hard cock sprang free. "Amuse yourself whilst we ride. Touch the part of me that will soon pierce your sweet, tight cunt."

Was Lucifer the warhorse or the man? Or did the name fit them both?

Rolfe's cock entranced her, the way it pulsed between his thick mail-clad thighs. His chain mail hauberk had a v-shaped slit that parted in the lush nest of hair that surrounded the base of his shaft and the heavy sac that held his seed.

When she noticed his cock bore armor, she suppressed the exclamation of surprise that hovered on her lips. Two pairs of bejeweled golden studs winked up at her from both sides of the scarred ridge where the bulging purplish head met a long, thick shaft. And a thick, glittering gold ring protruded from the underside of his cockhead and disappeared into a dimpled slit at the tip of his engorged flesh. Strange, yet arousing. But having the adornments implanted must have taken more fortitude than she could imagine.

When she took him in her hand and timidly handled the studs and ring, he smiled. "They'll not hurt you, sweeting, but give you pleasure the likes of which you've never known. Like you what you see?"

"Yes." He was so big. Silky smooth yet hard, he was the texture of velvet over steel. She imagined he would be like that all over, satin skin over flesh honed to muscular perfection on training field and battlefields, with a smattering of body hair the color of the dark nest from which his cock rose. "But your cock looks not like that of other men."

"I am circumcised."

"My lord?"

"I was captured in the East. An infidel doctor removed my foreskin." With one hand, he took her finger and traced it around the scar tissue around the base of his bulging cockhead.

"Oh."

Her womb wept for want of him, though fear rose in her, as he grew hotter, more formidable before her eyes. A creamy pearl of moisture glistened at the tip of his cock, translucent where it surrounded the gold ring and spilled over onto flesh the color and texture of a deep cabochon garnet.

His juice felt slick and alive when she rubbed it with her finger. She wanted to bend and taste it. Despite his words, she wanted to guide him to the spot between her legs that wept for him. She yearned to take his pulsating cock within her cunt and ride him as they rode the warhorse named Lucifer, until the ache inside her subsided.

"Cease your play, Jasmine. I will fuck you soon enough. We approach Hedgewick." Freeing his pulsing flesh from her hand, he adjusted his garments.

As Lucifer's massive hooves pounded against the wooden drawbridge, she stroked Rolfe through his braies. The thin fabric did little to disguise his readiness, naught to cool her lust for this mighty knight.

She knew not who she was or from whence she came, but she sensed that this man was her destiny. She would be his Jasmine, and she would capture his soul.

Chapter Two

In the back of Rolfe's lust-dulled mind the question lingered. Who was Jasmine and from whence had she come? Whoever she was, she'd captivated Rolfe with her beauty. And the sensual, carnal way she looked at him. He'd seek out answers as to who she was and how she'd happened to be on the road alone, unprotected by father, husband, or lover. Later.

Now all he wanted to do as he carried her up the steep stone staircase into Hedgewick's dismal hall was ease the ache she'd stoked to a fever pitch in his cock and balls. Fuck her until they both were so satiated they could fuck no more.

The hall looked even worse than he'd imagined it would. Rolfe doubted the rushes had been changed in the great hall since he'd been gone, considering the rancid smell that greeted him when he stepped inside the keep. Dust lay thick upon the raised dais, and smoke from burning fat wafted from the great fireplace where two servants turned a brace of hares upon a spit.

Prospects for a decent meal seemed slim. No matter. He'd take refuge in his solar now and deal with his inept steward and cowering servants after taking his fill of Jasmine. Later would be soon enough to chastise the serfs for neglecting their duties in his absence.

"You there. Fill my tub," he bellowed to a sturdy looking wench who sidled up to them when they came through the door. "And bring me wine, bread and cheese."

Scooping his beautiful stranger into his arms, Rolfe climbed the stairs to the solar. 'Twas fate, he decided, that he'd declined to wed with Lord Eudo's bitter-mouthed daughter. If he had stayed and married her, he'd not have chanced upon the treasure he now held.

Like the rich tapestries, precious books, and lush furnishings, Jasmine contributed to the luxurious surroundings of this, his private space. She made him feel as though he weren't a landless younger son and brother but rather a great lord.

He'd wrap himself in her silky raven hair, feast upon the rosy nipples that crowned full, creamy breasts. Drink of her honey and bury his cock to the hilt in her sopping cunt. Soon. 'Twas eagerness to claim her now that made him wave away his page and squire, and send the servants on their way as soon as they'd finished filling the tub and setting out a meager offering of food and drink.

When they were alone, he set Jasmine on her feet and lifted off the sling that held his broadsword within its leather scabbard. "Help divest me of my armor, sweeting."

She looked at him and smiled. "If you would seat yourself, my lord. You are too tall for me to lift off your hauberk while you stand." Jasmine's Norman French flowed naturally from her lips, and from her lack of hesitation when he asked her to relieve him of his mail, he assumed she'd performed that service for knights before.

Sitting on a stool as she'd requested, Rolfe lifted the hem of the heavy mail into her small, soft hands. Her skill at divesting him of the hauberk reinforced his belief that he'd claimed no peasant wench. Yet 'twas confusing, for she appeared as eager to fuck as he. More so. She'd practically devoured his cock as they galloped along the road.

Rolfe beat down the voice inside him that bade him send her to Hedgewick's other tower and find out who she was before making her his bed wench. He could not wait. From the way she caressed his balls once she'd stripped away his braies, he gathered her need was as great as his own.

The hot, eager look in her stormy eyes when she divested herself of his surcoat confirmed her lust. Sweeping her hip-length hair over her shoulder, she smiled a siren's smile. God's blood, but his cock was on fire. Having her would be worth whatever consequences might result. Of that he had no doubt. Once he was naked, he settled himself in the big oak tub. "Join me. There's room aplenty."

She stepped daintily into the water and settled before him on her knees, a pot of soft soap in one hand. "I would bathe you, my lord."

"And I you." Rolfe dipped two fingers into the pot, then rubbed the soap onto his hands.

Starting at the enticing column of her throat, he scoured away grime and brigands' blood from skin as soft as velvet. Unable to resist, he lowered his head and tasted her firm, full breasts. Her rosy nipples puckered against his tongue, became as hard as his throbbing cock.

He dipped his hands beneath the water and bathed her flat belly, slender thighs, and the sweet spot between them where he soon would find release. He found her pulsating clit and circled it with his thumb while working a finger into her incredibly tight cunt.

With eager hands, she soaped his body, circling his chest. Her fingers tangled in the hair that grew there and obscured the small rings embedded in his nipples. Then she slid her hands lower, soaped his belly and legs and feet. She was killing him! His balls drew up against his body.

His cock grew even longer and harder when she brought her hands closer and explored his seed sac with gentle curiosity. Then she closed both hands around his cock and ran a finger inside the ring that pierced its head. 'Twas all he could do to maintain control, for his balls felt as though they'd explode.

"Cease, sweeting. I would spill my seed within your tight, hot cunt, not in our bath water." He lapped droplets of water off her nipples, tasting the spicy, incredibly arousing warmth of her skin. Her needy whimpers drove him to increase the pressure of his fingers on her clit and in her cunt. Even in the water as they were, the flow of her hot, slick juices over his hand let him know he'd driven her to a frenzy of wanting.

Her own exploring fingers were driving him half-mad, and from the way she squirmed at his sensual onslaught, he deduced his touch inflamed her, too. "Why have you these adornments?"

"To bring you pleasure. They are common in the East." Rolfe fought back memories of the tortures inflicted upon him by an infidel prince, the evidence of which he'd chosen to mask with the golden cock ring. It had drawn shrieks of fear and disgust from some lovers, lascivious interest from others he'd bedded since returning from the Holy Land.

Her fingers gently rotating the ring through his swollen cockhead, Jasmine looked up at him. "Do they not cause you pain?"

"Nay. The wounds are well healed." Were they not, what she was doing would have been excruciating rather than arousing. "Come, sweeting, the water grows cold. Let us explore each other further in yonder bed."

Dry and naked, he lay back in the massive bed and watched her dry her hair. The thought of tangling it about his body, binding her to him with those silken ebony strands made his mouth go dry.

Jasmine looked her fill at the dark knight.

Her savior. Her fallen angel. The knight she'd dreamed of yet never imagined she'd e'er possess.

The bed linens, bleached white with age and many washings, contrasted with a coverlet of marten furs and his sun-kissed, lightly furred body.

His rampant cock stood erect, blue-veined and throbbing. The ring through its ruby tip reflected the flickering light from beeswax candles burning in silver sconces about the room. It held her gaze as though it had cast a warlock's spell upon her. Looking at him that way and imagining taking his huge sword deep inside her cunt made her love juices flow, wetting her with slick, hot liquid.

A sweet smell of incense permeated the air, and a breeze from the arrow slits took the edge off the white-hot heat of her desire.

"Come to me, Jasmine."

The deep sound of Rolfe's voice poured over her like honey and mead, sweet yet seductive, at once gentle and fierce. She sat on the edge of the bed and looked her fill at his handsome face…his massive, powerfully muscled body. A huge man, he bore few battle scars, but she recalled the apparent ease with which he'd dispatched her attackers and imagined he had left his mark on many an unfortunate knight. The pelt of dark hair on his broad chest narrowed to a thin line at his waist, then fanned out again to surround his huge, rigid cock.

She shuddered. That jeweled sword would soon pierce her, and though she wanted to take it deep within her cunt and feel its strength, she felt a frisson of unease.

"What if I am yet a virgin, my lord?" she whispered as she lay her head on his chest.

"I will take care, my sweet. If I must deflower you, 'twill hurt but for a moment, ere joy washes the pain away."

She shifted her head, and her lips came in contact with a pebbled nub. When she took his nipple in her mouth the way he had suckled her in the bath, she caught the small ring with her tongue. With one hand, she searched out and found his other flat male nipple, similarly raised at its tip by a thin gold ring that passed through his flesh.

"More gold, my lord?"

"'Tis usually a woman's adornment, but the rings can bring pleasure to a man, as well. Come, my Jasmine. Ride me as you would a mighty stallion." He lifted her at the waist, settled her astride him, and drew her down until their lips met.

'Twas carnal, all sensation and little else, the way he thrust his tongue into her mouth and sucked hers deep into his throat while he used his fingers to coax more of the slick juices from her throbbing cunt.

Rolfe inserted one finger inside her, his touch gentle as he probed her depths. "Sweeting, you will be mine alone," he murmured against her lips before sealing them to hers once more.

So no man's sword had yet pierced her. He would be the first. She clutched his shoulders, urging him ever closer. *Hurry, my dark angel.* Impatient, she wanted to beg him to rid her of her innocence. Show her carnal joys she had so far only glimpsed.

When he broke the kiss, she felt bereft. But then he shifted and positioned himself to enter her, and she rose on her knees to give him room. The feel of his hard, hot cock pulsing against her sopping inner lips, throbbing wildly and tipped with rigid gold, made her squirm. Made her yearn for more.

"Take my hands, sweeting." Arms extended at his sides, he entwined their fingers when she did his bidding.

She lay sprawled atop him, the hard, aching tips of her breasts stabbing his chest. The soft hair on his legs tickled her inner thighs, and the blunt, thick tip of his rigid cock pulsated as though knocking at the door to her soul. She needed all of him, wanted to take his hot flesh and fill the aching void inside her.

"'Tis the coitus of the gods." He shifted his hips and slid a fraction of an inch farther inside her.

She gasped. Stretching. Hot. Wet. Like a water lily in a pond, her body opened slowly yet distinctly enough that every contact, each nuance of sensation shimmered, spreading through her body and ohhh...

Beeswax and musky incense filled her nostrils and mingled with the heady scent of clean male flesh. His muscular neck tasted salty as fresh sea air when she sampled it with her tongue. The ring in one of his nipples gently abraded her shoulder. When a rumble of pleasure erupted from deep in his throat at the contact, she experienced a heady feeling of sensual power.

Power and surrender. Her surrender to his greater strength as he grasped her hands harder, his big callused fingers entwining with hers. Anchoring her in a compelling yet strange new world where all that mattered was satisfying the white-hot desire for him to quench the fire he'd ignited inside her.

He arched his hips and thrust upward. He tore through her maiden's barrier and buried his jeweled sword to the hilt. With his lips he captured her mouth and muffled her cries.

"The pain is done with, sweeting. You are mine. 'Twill be naught but pleasure now," he murmured as he kissed away her tears.

His obsidian eyes reflected the candles' glow and seduced her soul, as surely as his body possessed hers.

His hot gaze penetrated her, the passion there tempered with apparent concern. His big body shook, as though it took great effort for him to hold back. She sensed what his restraint cost in the tight line of his sensual mouth, the bulging muscles in his neck and outstretched arms. But the searing, stretching sensation where he filled her was almost too much to bear.

Then the pain gave way to wonder. A sensation of fullness, of heated male flesh throbbing within her body, taunted her with the unspoken promise that there was more to come. More than the delicious sensation of having his huge, hard cock buried within her, its strange adornments heightening her awareness and sending shards of pleasure deep into her core.

She strained to take more of him, but he shook his head. "Later we will explore passion's many pathways, my Jasmine. For now, let me lead the way."

With her thighs caressing his and their hands clasped and arms stretched outward, she lay still above him and savored each gentle thrust, striving for the ecstasy she sensed lay just outside her reach, until he stiffened beneath her and flooded her with his seed. She flexed her hips, wanting to take all of his massive length, but he rolled her over and disengaged their bodies, then spread her legs and rested his head between her thighs.

Alarmed, she tried to sit up, but he stilled her with a gentling touch. "Be not afraid, sweeting. I would drink at your fountain of love, that you may find the heights of joy you have just given me."

His hot breath tickled her thighs, ruffling the short soft hair that hid her secrets. She held her breath as he took her outer lips between his fingertips and pinched them together slowly, deliberately. With lips as soft as velvet he kissed the captured flesh, forcing his tongue through the opening to probe her trembling cunt.

Need bubbled within her. She rose against him seeking more. He drove his tongue in, then withdrew it, going deeper with each plunge. Slick, soft, sensual, his tongue soothed her while he ground his face against her slit, lightly abrading her sensitized flesh with his shadow of a beard. Embarrassed when she felt more juices gush from her cunt, she tried to slide away, but he held her fast.

What he was doing must surely be forbidden, but he seemed not to care.

He feasted on her. With every swipe of his tongue, each erotic scrape of his teeth against her cunt, he drove her higher. The pressure began where he suckled her around the swollen bud where her woman's pleasure centered. It spread, curling like an insistent flame low in her belly until it encompassed her. She gained temporary respite only when he paused now and then to sample the nectar that flowed from her womb.

When he took her nipples between his fingers and tugged them lightly, she burst amongst searing waves of pure pleasure.

He brought her down slowly, so slowly she thought she would die. Then, as though he were servant instead of master, he took a warm wet cloth and cleansed away her virgin's blood and his seed first from her tender flesh, then from his own still rigid cock.

* * * * *

She was more than he had dreamed of, all he had ever sought. Rolfe knelt between Jasmine's widespread thighs and cupped her firm, satiny buttocks.

Aroused again already at the sight of her spread warm and willing in his bed, he bent and probed her navel with his tongue. She tasted of sweet soap and salt. That taste fed his appetite. God's blood but he'd never get enough of her.

Her soft belly cradled his cheek. No peasant wench could be so creamy smooth, so exquisite. And no serf as beautiful as she would have been untouched. Guilt nagged at Rolfe. He should have withstood temptation, however eager she'd been to relinquish her virginity in his bed.

Then she ran her fingers through his hair and sighed. As though asking for something more, she rolled her hips upward toward his seeking mouth and, guilt or no, he was powerless to resist her invitation. He slid down her luscious body, tasting as he went, rotating his tongue in the archway to where the love-god dwelled.

Slowly, gently, he lapped her cunt, sampling the erotic juices. Her honey, his seed, flavored with the spices from their bath and her own womanly essence. His own lust dulled for the moment, he savored the tickling sensation of her pubic curls brushing his cheeks. The silky smoothness of her thighs.

He loved the way she grasped his head, urging him with little moans and whimpers to take her higher. "Yesss. Oh, yes, that feels so good," she hissed when he nibbled her clit and flailed it with his tongue. "Oh my Goddddd."

When she writhed with pleasure, he felt ten feet tall. Wanting to hold her, he lay beside her and gathered her in his arms. Surely she could want no more.

She reached down and stroked his cock with one hand. "Why did you not seek your own release again, my lord?" she asked, her expression curious.

"I would not hurt you, sweeting. Your honeypot needs gentle initiation, and I am not a small man. My cock can wait, for the pleasure it promises you is worth a few days' deprivation."

With one finger, she rotated the ring through his flesh, making him swell again to full erection. 'Twas good the damned thing appeared to fascinate rather than repel her. Unfortunately what she was doing had him hot to fuck her again. Closing his eyes, he made a futile effort to relax and go to sleep.

"I would do for you as you did for me." She smiled, then found one of his nipples and gave its ring a gentle tug. "May I give you pleasure?"

"You need not. I will survive." His cock twitched, as though to dispute what he'd just said.

Jasmine bent and wet his distended nipple with her tongue, then raised her head to meet his gaze. "You please me greatly. I wish to serve you, to learn how I may please you in every way, my lord."

"Rolfe." He had the sudden need to hear his name from her sweet lips.

"Rolfe. I wish to please you as you please me." Smiling, she bent again and caught one of his nipple rings between her teeth.

He found he could not say her nay, that whatever his beautiful Jasmine wished would be his command. "I am yours. Do as you will."

He caught a handful of her hair and brought it to his face to savor the sweet smell, the silky softness of her, before letting her slide down the bed and lie between his legs. He nearly came when she flicked her tongue along the underside of his cock while cupping his seed sac in both hands and squeezing gently.

"Like you this?" she asked.

He loved it. Loved feeling her breath, her warm slick tongue... He groaned.

She slid her hands upward, found his nipples, and tugged playfully at the sensitive nubs before rotating the rings slowly through his flesh. "This?" Her breath blew warm and damp against his straining sex.

It took all the self-control he could muster to keep from drawing her into his arms, spreading her legs, and driving himself hard and deep into her. If she were not a virgin just now deflowered...

"Oh God. Know you how your touch inflames me?"

"As yours does me, my lord."

She took the head of his cock in her mouth and sucked it, her tongue worrying first one, then the other of the pairs of beads an infidel healer had promised would restore the sensations lost when his captors had circumcised him. He'd been right. His balls tightened, and the pressure to let go built with every swipe of her tongue on his cockhead, each tug of her fingers on his nipples and the rings that pierced them.

He could take no more. Choosing the position least likely to cause her pain, he set her on her knees and pressed her breasts and forehead to the bed. Very carefully he positioned himself behind her, raised her buttocks, and guided his cockhead into her sweltering cunt.

When he moved in her, she moaned. Pleasure or pain? "Shall I stop?"

"Don't...stop. Fuck me, please fuck me."

He slid in deeper, until the tip of his cock touched her womb. The heat engulfed him, and it took all his self control not to rear back, ram her hard and fast until he found release. Instead, he paused. "Squeeze my cock."

"Yes, my lord. Oh, yessss." While he remained still inside her, she clenched him, milked him. The pressure in his balls intensified, then released as her sweet cunt sucked out his seed.

Chapter Three

Sunlight streamed through arrow slits in the solar, illuminating tapestries and jeweled chests that bespoke great wealth. Not altogether unpleasant aches reminded Jasmine how she and Rolfe had passed the night. She reached between her legs and stroked the sensitive flesh he'd awakened with such care and skill.

"Good morning, sweeting." He stood in the doorway to the solar, clad in a black velvet bed robe. His smile made him look young, almost boyish.

"My lord Rolfe."

"I would that you dispense with titles when we are alone. Besides, I am no lord, but merely the king's knight and vassal to my lord brother, the Earl of Harrow."

"But you possess great wealth." She glanced at rich tapestries on the wall, noticing that each depicted exotic looking couples engaged in various carnal acts, some of which she would have considered impossible before last night.

He sat beside her and swept back the covers, his hot gaze as arousing as his touch. "Most are treasures captured from the infidel. They are not nearly as precious as the prize you have given me." Gently, he lifted her hips and swept away the bloody linen.

"Rolfe?"

"Nay, sweeting. Were we wed, I would fly this prize from the castle tower. Since we are not, I shall keep it as a reminder of your most priceless gift."

We are not wed. Her throat tightened.

From somewhere within her faulty memory, she recalled feasting, raucous jests, a bride and groom stripped naked and put into the marriage bed by drunken guests. A great castle perched on the sea, and a laughing groom hoisting bloodied sheets like a pennon atop a square stone tower.

She pictured herself comforting a weeping bride.

Sensing his confusion at her sudden silence, she tried to explain. "'Tis naught but fractured images I see."

"Images? Tell me what you have seen."

"The wedding of a lord and lady. I know not whom or when or where. But I saw them plainly, in a castle by the sea."

"Mayhap your memory will return. From your speech and manner, sweeting, I'd wager you're no peasant wench." With his free hand, Rolfe stroked her cheek. His smile heated her blood when he glanced at the stained linen in his hand. "From this, I'd wager you were not the bride."

He strode to the chest nearest the window and laid the folded linen within, then lifted a smaller cask and brought it to the table beside the bed. His dark eyes nearly black as he looked upon her, he sat and drew out what looked like a string of large pink pearls.

Bending, he kissed her breasts, then drew a tingling nipple into his mouth and flailed it with his tongue. Need stirred in her belly, and she moaned pitifully when he gave a gentle nip and raised his head.

But when he moved lower and nudged her legs apart, she forgot the cold sensation of loss in her nipple. Yes! His mouth felt like heaven when he brushed it along her slit. When he sucked the aching kernel of her passion, she writhed beneath him, wanting more. Wanting him. She looked at him as she plunged her fingers into his silky sable hair.

The sight of him loving her that way in the light of day, his dark head bent to her cunt as if in supplication, the feel of his hot breath and velvet tongue bathing her most secret places, took her breath away.

Sensations banished the melancholia that had o'ertaken her when she realized she'd never be more than leman to her noble knight. When he parted her inner lips with gentle fingers and slid the pearls deep into her sheath, her love juices flooded his hand. Unlike his searing hot flesh, the pearls felt cool and smooth inside her.

"Keep these snug within your warm, tight sheath, my Jasmine. I will remove them ere we make love again."

Jasmine tightened her inner muscles, felt a pang of pure sexual longing when the pearls shifted within her vagina. "Then remove them now, my lord, for my womb cries for you."

"Nay. You need time to heal from your deflowering. I could tear you asunder should I fuck you the way I yearn to, ere you are healed. I should not have given in to my lust and taken you a second time last eve."

He loosened his robe, lifted his half-hard cock by the ring at its tip. "The waiting is a price I must pay for being as large as I am, especially since I wear this. I would not hurt you."

She wanted him inside her now. Welcomed any pain his huge jeweled cock might cause. 'Twas all Jasmine could do not to straddle him and impale herself upon it. Perhaps if he—"Can you not remove the ring?"

"Nay. 'Tis welded on. Only when the opening stretches enough that it needs be replaced with a thicker ring do I have my armorer remove it." He reached inside the cask and withdrew a handful of smooth gold open links in varying diameters and graduated thicknesses. The smallest looked slightly thicker than the one now sealed through the head of his cock. "You may choose my next ring to suit your pleasure, sweeting."

Then, he looked down at himself and, with two fingers, grasped one of the studs. "I can remove these, but I seldom do, since 'tis the devil's own task to put them back. I have more of them, should you like the feel of them within your body."

The little ball Rolfe held was fastened to the ridge where his shaft flared out into a plumlike head. A thin gold post apparently passed through a narrow wedge of his flesh and was attached on the other side to a matching one. The studs were held securely to the post in a manner much like the way her earrings fastened to her ears.

Earrings? Jasmine felt her earlobes. There were no jewels there, yet she distinctly remembered a needle's sting, the weight of glittering jewels she'd always hated to hide beneath a lady's wimple.

"I wore earrings once," she murmured, feeling with her fingertips the ridge on the backside of one ear.

Rolfe took her earlobe between his teeth and searched it with his tongue. Then he cupped her breasts with his callused hands and met her gaze. "I feel the holes where you were pierced. Mayhap your attackers stole your jewels. The remnants of your garments were those of a peasant and your naked beauty dazzled me so much, I thought not to search the bodies. Would you that I send some men at arms to do so now?"

"Nay." Instinct told her much time had passed since she'd lived with the kind of luxury that surrounded her now. With costly trinkets like the pearls he had just placed within her body to facilitate her pleasure and his.

"How will you remove the pearls?" she asked, not willing to test her faulty memory further than last night, when he'd brought her pleasure beyond any she had ever imagined.

"Like this." He spread her legs wide with both hands, and rested the heel of his hand on her tingling love button while he dipped one long finger deep inside her cunt and retrieved the pearls. The smooth, hard spheres brushed the walls of her cunt, releasing more juices to flood his fingers.

"Or like this." When he slid the jewels back inside, it was as though she consciously sucked them in. She felt full, almost as full as when she'd taken his huge cock into her body. Deliciously full. Then he replaced his hand with his lips and sucked upon her until the pearls slipped out of her cunt into his mouth. When he'd pushed them as far inside her as he could reach with his tongue, he kissed his way up her body. Her juices glistened hot and slick over his cheeks and lips where he'd pressed his face against her swollen labia.

"Taste your honey, my sweet," he said when he lifted his head and met her gaze.

The sweet-salty love juice on his lips and tongue was not unpleasant. Mingled as it was with a hint of mulled wine and Rolfe's own unique taste, the taste made her want more.

His cock throbbed hard against her belly, and his crisp body hair tickled her sensitized flesh. Certain when she returned his kiss that he would ease the wanting he had created, she cried out when he stood and donned his bed robe. "My lord, I need you now to ease this longing. Please."

"Cease, Jasmine. While I'd gladly pleasure you all day, I needs must put to order this cursed keep. My steward is a lazy fool, and without a lady to order the servants, they do naught when I am away. You are welcome to stay here in the solar where 'tis passably clean, or go below, as you will."

Jasmine climbed down from the big bed. The pearls slid down when she stood, forcing her to tighten her inner muscles to hold them inside.

Rolfe paused while tying plain brown woolen braies about his narrow waist. "You will soon become accustomed to the feel of the pearls, sweeting. 'Twill strengthen your inner muscles to clasp them tightly within you as you go about the keep, and I am told that they give a lady great pleasure when she rides her palfrey. When you milk my cock with your cunt the way you will milk the pearls, 'twill give me joy beyond any you can imagine."

"I would go below, my lord, but I have no clothing."

His gaze scorched her, while his smile warmed her heart. "I will send a woman with whatever ladies' raiment may be found. For now you may ward off the chill with this."

She watched the heavy door close behind him, then wrapped her aching body in the velvet bed robe he'd handed her. When she spied an open book that lay on a bench below the shuttered window, she picked it up and glanced at the erotic drawings, all the while clasping and relaxing her inner muscles around the pearls as Rolfe had bade her to do.

A pleasant glow began to radiate throughout her body as she studied the exquisite drawings of couples pleasuring each other in ways she'd never even imagined. Soon her cunt wept more hot, slick juices as she clenched her inner muscles around the smooth warm jewels. 'Twas as if they reminded her that passage was meant to be filled—fucked by her lord Rolfe's big, jeweled cock in the many ways she saw from the arousing drawings that other men fucked their partners.

* * * * *

Jasmine had just begun to study a highly arousing drawing of three men pleasuring one lucky lady when Rolfe returned to the solar.

Hot juices bathed her slit at the sight of her handsome lover, and she let his bedrobe slip off her shoulders. "Welcome, my lord," she said, going to her knees and fumbling with the ties to his braies.

"Would that I could stay, sweeting. I've been summoned to do battle for my lord brother. I come only to arm myself ere I ride out."

"I would help you." Rising, she fought down the lust that made her want to shove him to the bed and take her pleasure, and instead watched him lay out his armor.

From what he told her, she surmised that a messenger had just arrived, bringing word that a cousin of Harrow's former lord was attacking Harrow, seeking to oust Lord Giles and take what he considered his birthright.

"I would that you think of me whilst I am gone, sweeting," Rolfe said as she helped him don his padded gambeson and chain mail hose. "I know not how long this will take, so if you will lie on the bed for a moment, I will remove the pearls."

He withdrew them, then bent and tongued her cunt for just a moment before kneeling and handing her his hauberk. As she helped lift his heavy chain mail shirt over his head, the warm trickle of love juices down her inner thighs cried out for the man she'd soon be watching ride away.

"God grant you safety and a quick victory, my lord," she murmured once his armor was in place. Truly she wanted him to stay so she could strip him naked and entice him into her arms again.

Rolfe looked surprised at the formal benediction, but he bent and brushed his lips across hers before giving the traditional reply. "'Twill be so. My lord brother's cause is just."

When he picked up his helm and tucked it under one arm, Jasmine glanced down at herself. "I would bid you farewell in the bailey, but I've naught to wear."

"I ordered one of the maids to find some ladies' garb. She will soon bring you whatever may be found in this wretched keep."

"Thank you, my lord. I would be pleased to make myself useful during your absence if you wish it."

Rolfe smiled. "I'd have you take the place in hand whilst I am gone. I've ordered old Martin, my steward, to obey you. 'Tis obvious from the disorder I saw on my return that he has neither the wit nor the will to rule the servants in my absence. I wager you'll do better."

"I will do my best, my lord. Your men await you. God go with you." Stretching on tiptoes, Jasmine brushed a gentle kiss across Rolfe's lips.

Soon afterward, she watched from the solar window as Rolfe departed with most of his men at arms. In full armor upon the young destrier named Lucifer, he made an impressive sight.

The picture of a perfect lover. A perfect love?

Nay. Not while she knew not who she was or from whence she had come. Not when she had neither estates nor riches to bring her fine knight.

Murmuring a prayer the words for which poured from somewhere in the deep recesses of her mind, Jasmine watched him ride away before setting about to do his bidding.

* * * * *

Ordering servants too long left to their own devices occupied her days, but each night Jasmine retired to feast her eyes on the sensual treasures in Rolfe's luxurious solar. The tapestries upon the wall held her attention and made her yearn to experience the sorts of pleasure so evident upon the faces of the lovers while they explored unfamiliar ways of loving. The drawings in the richly bound book Rolfe kept open upon a table by the bed, which she studied by the light of flickering candles, fed carnal desires that grew stronger every day.

When the candles guttered, she lay in the dark, aching…yearning…desperate to experience more of the pleasure Rolfe had shown her. She dreamed of partaking of those erotic, forbidden joys depicted in the pictures within his precious book and upon the exotic tapestries.

One night she inserted the pearls the way he'd done, but that only made the longing worse. Needing to ease the yearning, she rolled her tingling nipples until they rose in rigid little points against the furs—furs that caressed her naked skin almost as though they had life of their own. She found the pleasure spot he'd shown her and circled it with a finger until it hardened and throbbed. Until her juices flowed hot and thick and copiously. And once, out of desperation, she removed the pearls and inserted two fingers into her sopping, throbbing cunt.

'Twas a damned poor substitute for Rolfe's huge, jeweled sword…or his mouth that brought such pleasure when he used it on her joy button. Even his callused fingers would have done more for her than her own.

Desperate for release, she inserted another finger and pressed her palm hard against her throbbing clit. Finally. Relief. But not joy or satisfaction. Jasmine counted the hours until Rolfe would return, for only he could give her what she needed.

* * * * *

On the fifth day of his absence, a messenger came. The siege was over, the attackers vanquished. Rolfe was unhurt, the man told her, and he would return soon—as soon as a christening could be arranged at Harrow for his brother's newborn heir.

Jasmine looked about the hall the day before Rolfe's expected return. Not without difficulty, she'd managed to establish her rule and order his servants to clean and lay new rushes. Old Martin deserved not the title of steward, for he did naught but laze about the hall while the servants had done as they would until she demonstrated that failure to obey would result in swift, painful consequences.

She watched with satisfaction while two servants whitewashed the sooty wall above the wide open hearth and another maid scoured the high table where Rolfe would eat. Finally the hall was clean, but it certainly looked shabby compared with her lover's luxuriously appointed solar. Pity she could do no more with the tools at hand. Ascending the narrow curved stair, Jasmine looked forward to a bath, and to studying yet another page of Rolfe's erotic picture book.

In the large oaken tub where she and Rolfe had bathed together before he'd shown her paradise, Jasmine let warm water lap against her while she inhaled the steamy scent of roses from the oil she'd massaged into her breasts and belly. As she stroked her slick skin and inhaled the warm, moist fragrance, she wished he were here. Especially when her motion set the water to lapping softly against the weathered wood, caressing her sex with its undulating motion.

She sighed and dipped her head, wetting her hair, then rubbed soft soap through the sopping strands.

How gentle had been his touches, how different they had been from the—

Suddenly cold despite the water's warmth, she tried again to remember.

What memory could she have almost triggered by soaping her hair?

No matter. With Rolfe she would make new memories, sensual memories that would last a lifetime if whomever she had been fleeing should find her and lock her away.

Jasmine would not try to recall how she came to be alone in the forest of Harrow, for she sensed she had been running from something that would hurt too much to recall. She would mourn not for memories that weren't worth her grief, but take pleasure in the present and the sensual possibilities in her future as Rolfe's leman.

Concentrating on her bath and the sensations that surrounded her, she closed her eyes and rubbed her hands over her aching body. In her mind she pictured her fallen angel and yearned for his return. Yearned for his tongue to soothe her aching nipples, for his mighty cock to fill all her empty, weeping places…some still virgin but eager for his erotic initiation.

* * * * *

As soon as the baptism was over, Rolfe gathered his troop and rode out of Harrow. Twelve days was too long to have spent without a woman to warm his bed. Too long to have endured without drinking in the sight and feel of Jasmine.

As he and his men galloped past the clearing where he had found her, his excitement rose. Leaving the others far behind, he spurred Lucifer and made for Hedgewick.

For Jasmine.

He arrived in the hour before dawn, a thick coating of dust from the road upon him and his mount. Exhaustion warred with unslaked passion—and lost.

No other woman had ever enticed Rolfe the way Jasmine did. No other had ever ruined his taste for Harrow's fulsome wenches, who had been as quick as usual to offer themselves for his pleasure. No other woman had ever made him so eager to fuck her that he'd have risked his destrier and his life the way he'd just done, to ride hell-bent through the night to her for no better reason than to ease the dull, persistent ache in his balls.

When he stepped inside and wakened a servant to divest him of his armor, he noticed the hall appeared uncommonly clean. "I see old Martin has finally taken the keep in hand," he commented.

The servant snorted. "Not Martin, my lord. 'Twas the lady Jasmine's doing."

Rolfe opened the solar door and spied her, curled up like a kitten in the middle of his bed. She must have been sleeping deeply, for he'd not been especially quiet in his haste to see her.

Who was this woman who'd enchanted him?

Though none passing through Harrow had spoken of a missing daughter or bride, Rolfe found it hard to believe any man would let a prize such as Jasmine slip from his grasp.

"Who are you, sweeting?"

Jasmine had captured his heart as well as his body. He would fight to the death to keep her. He would even wed her if he had not the need for land and titles.

He peeled away his dusty garments, then ran his fingers through his tangled hair while he watched her sleep.

The tub in the corner still held water from her bath.

Grateful to wash off the grime of the road although he shivered in the cold water, Rolfe caught a scent of roses. The fragrant oil left his skin slick, made him eager to run his hands and mouth over every inch of his sleeping prize.

Her tight little cunt should be healed now, he thought when he stretched out beside her and stroked along her sleek, damp slit. Rolfe felt her love juices begin to flow, saw her sleepy smile in the flickering flames of the fragrant candles that had lit his way to her.

"Awaken, my sweet," he whispered against her silky throat.

Her eyelids fluttered, then opened. An expression of joy washed over her face as she reached up to encircle him with eager arms. "My lord. Your messenger told me to expect you on the morrow."

"I could not wait. Cannot wait. Open your legs for me."

Like a flower unfurling from a bud into full bloom, she clasped her arse cheeks with her hands and opened her thighs wide. When she dug her heels into the bed beside her slim hips, he positioned himself at love's door and took her beautiful breasts in his hands.

"You have been studying the tapestries, my Jasmine." He slid his cock inside her silken sheath.

She smiled. "And your book. With you away, my lord, 'twas naught to do but dream, imagine how your great cock would fill me when you came home. I made myself wet contemplating the many ways we would bring each other pleasure."

She shifted her hips, took him deeper, contracted and relaxed her inner muscles, coaxing out his seed. Stealing his resolve to make this last. His restraint destroyed, he braced his hands beside her face and fucked her hard.

"My lord, I prayed for your return. Needed you. Needed this. Oh, yesss." Her soft moans inflamed him, encouraged him to go faster. The urgency in his balls intensified, spread, threatened to ignite.

When she brought her soft thighs higher and wrapped her ankles around his shoulders, he could hold out no longer. One mighty thrust seated him in her to his balls. Letting go, he spurted his hot seed deep into her tight, pulsating cunt.

He didn't know how long he stayed in her, for his orgasm robbed him of reason. Eventually he rolled onto his side, his cock still nestled inside the mystery woman who had already come far toward stealing his heart.

Hours later sunlight was peeking through the arrow slits when he felt her wriggle out of his arms and leave the bed. This time it was she who returned with a soft, warm cloth with which she bathed his wrung-out cock and balls.

And 'twas she who lifted the jeweled lid to the chest beside the bed and smiled when she drew out a soft, white ostrich plume.

Chapter Four

The days passed quickly, the only blight on Jasmine's joy being the uncertainty of who and what she was. Fleeting, hazy memories plagued her, though they did naught to establish who she was or how she'd come to be traveling alone the day Rolfe had found her.

Harrow's servants did long-neglected chores under her watchful eye by day while Rolfe trained with his men. And when evening came they explored the varied ways to pleasure she'd seen illustrated in the infidel's picture book of sexual delights.

As she knelt before the fire in the solar one damp, chilly night while Rolfe combed the tangles from her flowing hair, a terrifying memory reared up from the deep recesses of her brain.

A bloody dagger...the last vestiges of a young woman's crowning glory tumbling onto the floor beneath her and mingling with the bloody locks of others who had gone before. More women kneeling on a cold stone floor with their shorn heads bowed. Their alabaster scalps dripped blood as they waited to be handed the wimples and veils that would hide their shame.

She shuddered when Rolfe laid down the comb and burrowed his long, callused fingers through the heavy strands of her hair. "Think you I might have been a holy nun?" Visions of hellfire and damnation ran rampant through her head.

"You're no nun, sweeting. But you tremble like a leaf in the wind. What troubles you?" Rolfe pulled her to her feet and wrapped her in the secure cocoon of his embrace.

If only she could see more than mere snatches from the past...these disjointed visions that made no sense. Haltingly, she related to him all she had just now remembered: the cold, dank place. Of new brides of Christ wearing rough homespun robes, kneeling on a hard stone floor while a forbidding, dour-faced nun scraped away their hair. "I have no vocation," she told him, her voice still shaky though he'd dispelled the chill in her bones with his nearness.

"That, my love, is obvious. No holy sister would take so readily to earthly pleasures. Perhaps you once attended the taking of vows as a guest. Come. Forget the disquieting vision and look at the picture book. Show me the scene that fires your blood this night, and then we will prove yet again that you were made for me and not the Church."

Jasmine followed him to the window and opened the book to the page with a drawing that had titillated her since first she saw it. A woman lay between two men, one fucking her cunt and the other her ass while she sucked upon the tongue of the man she faced.

"Like that, my lord," she told him, certain her cheeks were glowing in the dim candlelight though her cunt clenched and gushed out its juices at the thought of experiencing such complete fulfillment.

As though shocked, he stared at the pictures. "You are sure, sweeting?"

"Aye. Fill me completely, that I may drive away the demons in my poor addled brain," she told him. "You are but one man and I would have no other, but..."

"You'd have your mouth and cunt and even your puckered asshole filled with cocks and tongues? Though I am greedy and loath to share you with another man, I would please you." Rolfe yanked on the bell pull, then stared again at the drawing in which a woman rode one man's cock and consumed his mouth with her own while another man knelt between their legs and enthusiastically fucked her ass.

"Send Sir Alfred to me," he snapped at the sleepy serf who answered his summons.

Jasmine imagined the big, rawboned young knight who was captain of Rolfe's guard, the thought bringing none of the anticipation that coursed through her veins when she fantasized about having Rolfe invade her body. When she looked again at the drawing she let her thoughts transform her, carry her to a silk-draped divan in a strange, exotic land where lovers had no shame...where they continually devised new, erotic games to enhance their pleasure. Where no act was unthinkable if it produced the all-consuming, mind-altering sensations she'd experienced more strongly with every shattering climax.

"What think you, sweeting?" Rolfe asked, the golden adornments in his huge, rigid cock glittering in the firelight when he shed his bedrobe.

"I think I was made for your pleasure. Does the thought of sharing me with your vassal arouse you?" She loved the way his seed sac drew up close to his body and his shaft quivered when he wet his hand with the juices from her sopping cunt and used the slick, hot fluid to lubricate his swollen cockhead.

"If I had two cocks, Sir Alfred would not be joining us in heaven tonight, my sweet. Your sweet cunt belongs to me alone, but I am too greedy to let him take the virginity of your pretty ass. Get on your hands and knees on the bed."

When she did, she felt not Rolfe's ringed cock but his big hands spreading her ass cheeks and his velvety tongue ringing the entrance to the rear passage she'd evacuated and cleansed earlier while he lingered in the hall with his men. Her cunt clenched with excitement—and no small degree of fear, for she imagined his huge purple head splitting her ass asunder...anticipated pain far worse than when he'd breeched her maidenhead.

More slick, hot honey poured from her slit, over the rigid nub of flesh Rolfe now nibbled while he slid first one sopping finger, then two into her virgin hole. With his other hand he reached beneath her and pinched her nipples to rock-hard pleasure points. When she whimpered and begged him for more, he rolled her over to give him better access to her honey.

Rolfe sucked her clit while he finger-fucked her ass and tweaked her nipples with nimble fingers. Then he tongue-fucked her cunt until she shattered in a kaleidoscope of sexual sensation. He repositioned her on her hands and knees while her body shook with the intensity of her climax. The searing pain that followed when he eased his huge cock up her tight rear passage seemed trifling when compared with the orgasmic waves that were coursing through her body.

But the sensation of his hot wet seed spurting into her there triggered another wave of pleasure that left her limp and barely conscious.

How full she'd feel with two great cocks inside her, thrusting and pulsating and shooting out their seed in concert. The thought had her quim quivering with anticipation.

And... Nay, she wanted not another man, even though Sir Alfred was comely and the thought of being so filled titillated her senses. Only Rolfe.

Who didn't want to share her with another man. She wished to please him...and him alone. "My lord?"

He stirred, his beautiful dark eyes opening slowly to meet her gaze. "Yes?"

"About that picture..."

"I'd hear no more about it now. Rest." He rolled away, then got up as though troubled.

She dared not speak further, for from somewhere in the depths of her mind came the knowledge that one did not cross a man when he spoke thusly.

* * * * *

By all that was holy, he'd kill any other who sampled his woman. He'd allow none but himself to invade her silken flesh. Not even to enhance her pleasure. Rolfe watched Jasmine resting upon the furs on his bed while he used a soft, soapy rag to cleanse his cock and its adornments.

When Alfred knocked gently upon the solar door, Rolfe sent him away as he rifled through his collection of sexual toys looking for a blown-glass mushroom and the matching, eerily realistic dildo he'd purchased not long after his rescue from the infidel who'd held him. The bazaar had been teeming with exotically dressed men and veiled women trailed by their eunuch protectors.

At the time he'd thought the exotic toys might soon be his only possessions that could fill a woman's cunt. Rolfe shuddered at the memory of his imprisonment and the months that followed when he woke each day to agonizing pain and the fear that the infidel surgeon who tended his wounds would give up trying to heal him and cut away his tortured manhood.

He laid the toys on the bed and dipped his fingers into a squat ruby-glass pot filled with the magical aphrodisiac cream an ancient crone had sold him in the bazaar. Its musky fragrance filled the room, and when he used some to anoint his cock and balls a hot, urgent need kindled and spread even though he'd spilled his seed moments earlier. Then he scooped up another measure of the aphrodisiac and knelt between Jasmine's luscious thighs.

"I am sorry, sweeting, but I'll not share you with another man. Not even my closest comrade in arms," he murmured against her sweat-soaked buttocks moments later as he worked the cream along her slit, over the tight bud of her desire, into her dripping cunt, and finally around the puckered rosebud that protected her rear entrance.

"I do not mind. You are more than enough man for me."

She lifted her ass, and he couldn't resist bending to nip the plump pale flesh whilst he worked the well-lubricated mushroom past her anal sphincter until its flat iridescent foot rested flush against her slit.

"Ooh," she said, wiggling her hips as if to acquaint herself with the unfamiliar sensation of the cold, smooth glass inside her tight rear passage.

"Picture us in a seaside villa, on a silken couch. Date palms swaying outside the open window, and your personal eunuch arousing you for me with his hands and mouth and sensual toys like these." Rolfe rubbed the dildo along her hot, swollen slit.

Her eager cunt gushed its sweet, hot juices, inviting him to nibble the quivering, rock-hard nub beyond it. Her moan when he tongued her there reminded him of how she devoured his cock with her pretty mouth, the sensation of her darting tongue on his distended flesh, her hot wet breath tickling his balls while she sucked him deep in her throat and coaxed out his seed.

"May your eunuch drink of your honey? Fill your weeping cunt with this replica of your master's great cock?" Then he tongued her again, lapping up more of her slick, hot honey.

"Oh, yesss. Fill me. Fill all of me. Please. Give me your seed."

Carefully, Rolfe rolled her to her back. "Your eunuch has no seed. No cock. If he did your master would never let him near his precious jewel. But fear not. Your eunuch will fill you with this."

He eased the beautifully crafted dildo into her sopping cunt until its flared base rested against her labia. With his hands he spread her thighs wide apart while he straddled her face. And when she dug her fingers into his ass cheeks and dragged him down until his cock sank into her open mouth, he tensed with the effort of holding back his climax.

"Like that. Oh, yesss." He groaned when she took him deeper in her throat, swallowing convulsively around his cockhead while she cradled his balls and used her tongue to trace the prominent vein that ran up the underside of his shaft.

Wanting to enhance the sensual torture that already had her thighs quivering, he bent his head and blew gently on the glistening nub that begged for his mouth as he looked his fill at her drenched, swollen slit, held open by the bases of the rare glass toys that stretched and filled her cunt and the puckered hole whose virginity he'd taken with his cock moments earlier.

Rolfe had never seen anything so erotic as the vivid blues and reds, stained glass disks surrounded by the glistening pinkness of her slit and her lightly furred outer lips. Those lips pouted as he worked the dildo deep into her cunt and withdrew it, dripping with her fragrant, milky juices.

When he nestled his head between her thighs and feasted on her steaming nectar, she sucked him deeper down her throat. Her swallowing motions sent waves of pleasure down his spine, into his balls, and down his cock.

He'd never before filled a woman so completely. Never had one swallow his cock so sweetly while he fed on her honey and used his toys to fuck her cunt and ass in tandem. Power. 'Twas a heady feeling.

Damn. She took him even deeper, Her breath tickled his balls. He wanted to hold out, keep savoring the intense pleasure. But he couldn't withstand her erotic onslaught. He was coming.

He wanted her to come with him. Sliding the dildo deeper, then withdrawing it until its ruby head nestled within her pouting cunt lips, he took her hard nub between his teeth and flailed it with his tongue. When he slid the dildo back in, he felt the ripples of her climax in his fingers and his tongue, and in the convulsive swallowing motions of her throat around his spurting cock.

* * * * *

"Tell me about your time in the East," Jasmine murmured hours later while she lay in Rolfe's embrace and looked at the odd toys with which he'd filled her so completely. Sitting as they were upon the chest by the bed, they glowed red and blue and creamy white in the flickering light of a single candle. "And tell me more about these eunuchs who exist to bring women pleasure but who have no cocks or balls."

Idly Rolfe stroked her breast, rubbing a callused finger over the nipple. "Eunuchs are made by the slavers, for it is against the faith of the infidels to make eunuchs. The slaves who live through their gelding are brought to the markets. The complete eunuchs—those who have lost their cocks as well as their seed sacs—bring high prices as harem keepers for the wealthiest of the infidel princes."

Jasmine shuddered. "I'd not want such pain inflicted on any man to enhance my pleasure, or to deprive a lover of joy such as what you must feel when you spurt your seed into my body."

"The purpose of a harem eunuch is not to pleasure the women but to guard them and ensure the masters that any children born to their women have come from their seed. Any pleasure the eunuchs bring the women in their care is tolerated—even encouraged—for powerful infidel men keep many women, so many they may never lay eyes on them all."

"How came you to possess a eunuch's tools?" she asked, her gaze settling on his softened cock that rested peacefully against his prominent hipbone. "'Tis a fact you're no eunuch. A fact for which I am most grateful."

"When I was eleven years old I went to the East as my brother's squire. The infidel prince who captured me about a month after we'd arrived ordered me chained to the dungeon wall by my cock and nipples. His plan was that when the wounds festered, he would have me made a eunuch to preserve my life, which apparently is not a violation of their religious laws. Fortunately my brother freed me ere my wounds festered beyond repair, but 'twas not known for a time whether the wound from the piercing of my cock would heal. 'Twas thought the only way to save my life might be to make me a eunuch. I bought the toys in the bazaar of Constantinople because I feared they'd soon be my only means for pleasuring a woman. And I insisted that the rings my captors had put through my nipples not be removed even though the piercings there had healed, because for a eunuch, 'tis said the nipples are the only sources of sexual pleasure."

"I am glad you kept this," she said, leaning down to give his ringed cock a tender kiss. "Though the pain..." Jasmine shuddered when she imagined how Rolfe must have hurt when they'd forced the molten metal through his most sensitive flesh.

"'Tis all right, sweeting. 'Twas long ago and all I lost was my foreskin. I gained much knowledge of the ways to pleasure, along with the pain and these metal reminders of how close I came to becoming the eunuch slave of that infidel prince's favorite wife."

When Jasmine slept in Rolfe's arms that night, a vision came to her. Cloaked in a haze, a boy lay near death in an unfamiliar solar upon a richly carved bed while shadowy figures watched over him. A maiden, richly gowned and veiled as befit a grand lady, stepped out of the shadows, apparently wishing to give comfort and add her prayers to those being muttered by a wizened monk.

The boy moved—no, 'twas a man full grown, she realized as the haze lifted and allowed her a clearer vision. He lay naked, as still as death again, chalky pale upon the bloodied linen. Suddenly the stoop-shouldered warrior who stood vigil beside the bed turned on the woman.

"Take her," he said. "My heir lives. God has answered my prayers and she will be my offering of thanksgiving."

A journey. Long, arduous, slow, the litter in which the woman rode boxed her in, confined her. Jasmine sensed her pain, her fear, the terror that fueled her scream when the knights who'd made up her escort finally handed her kicking and screaming through a forbidding stone curtain wall into the keeping of a sinister, disembodied voice.

When Jasmine woke, sweat poured from her trembling body, and her knuckles shone white from the death grip she had on Rolfe's muscular shoulders.

"'Twas as though I'd glimpsed my own horror...my past," she sobbed when he pried her hands away and enfolded her in his strong arms.

Chapter Five

☙

"In time you will remember, sweeting," Rolfe told her a few days later as they rode through Hedgwick's gates, an escort following some distance behind. He hated the fear in Jasmine's beautiful eyes, the faint lines of exhaustion that ringed her mouth after yet another night of disjointed dreams, another day of not knowing who she was. And 'twas clear she'd not be happy until they solved the mystery.

Part of him wanted to keep her memories shrouded, for he sensed her reality would cause her more pain than the upsetting visions she'd been having more often these past few days. But she wanted to remember...needed to face whatever had made her flee, and put an end to the uncertainty that plagued her.

"Whoever I am, I do not wish to leave you." She tightened her hold on his waist when he set the old warhorse he'd chosen for them to ride into an easy gallop across the meadow.

"You will not, for I will never let you go." Ever. No matter to whom you may belong. Rolfe let go his grip on the horse's reins and squeezed her hand, tamping down the niggling fear in his gut that Jasmine might belong to one more powerful than he.

"Do you not need to hold the reins?"

"Rajah responds to the touch of my knees and heels, and to my spoken commands." At that moment a hare crossed their path, but the old destrier paid it no heed. "He carried me home from the Holy Land. Took some arrows in his shoulder at the siege of Harrow. Now he lazes in the meadow and impregnates my mares, but I'd still trust him with my life. Our lives. Should you wish it, perhaps you may ride me while we both ride Rajah later, when we are not likely to be seen by all."

"I would like that greatly." Jasmine leaned forward, brushing her lips against the back of his neck as she slid her hands down and caressed his cock and balls.

"Cease, sweeting, lest I stop now, mount you before me, and fuck your sopping little cunt in plain sight of Sir Alfred and the others. Look. There is where you were when I found you. In that clearing just ahead."

"I was here? Alone?" she asked, as though disbelieving that she had truly traveled through the dense deserted wood without escort. He felt a shudder go through her as he lifted her down from Rajah's back.

The memory of seeing the filthy brigands' hands and mouths on her made Rolfe's blood boil. "Yes," he told her through clenched teeth as he searched the ground for any sign that might remain to link her...anywhere.

Nothing. Not a shred of cloth, a stray bauble. Not that he'd expected to find anything. He trusted his men to have looked thoroughly when they'd stayed behind to bury the bodies of Jasmine's attackers. "Does this place bring back any memories?"

Her expression sad, she shook her head. Then she smiled. "I remember waking to see you staring down at me. And you wrapping me in your surcoat and setting me upon your great black destrier."

"You knew not the men who attacked you?"

"Nay. At least I don't think so." Her nose wrinkled, as though the stench of the unwashed bastards still hung in the warm spring air. "I'm sorry."

"'Tis all right. I'd hoped…"

"What is near here?" she asked.

Rolfe remembered the nearby cloister, and Jasmine's panic a few days earlier when she'd visualized what he gathered was a taking of nuns' vows. Could she…

No. He'd not risk frightening her again. "The land for miles around is part of Harrow," he told her, feeling no guilt for having neglected to mention the forbidding Convent of St. Benedict that sat beyond a bend in the road, less than a mile from where they stood. "Harrow Castle lies less than a day's ride to the east."

"You are certain I did not come from there?"

Rolfe shook his head. "I had my lord brother make inquiries. No one has reported a missing beauty with raven hair and eyes a man could drown in." Lowering his head, he took her mouth as he drew her lush body close. "Do not despair, sweeting. You are my gift from the angels," he murmured when she looked up at him.

"I cannot remember. Rolfe, make me forget everything but the pleasures we share."

He could not deny her. Not when she wet lips still swollen and reddened from sucking him to completion this morning. Nay, he could deny this woman nothing.

After setting her up onto Rajah's saddle, leaving both her legs draped over the horse's side, he reached up and ran a hand along her firm, shapely thigh, his balls tightening painfully when she spread her legs and bared her cunt to his gaze. It glistened in the sunlight that filtered through the branches above them, all pink and wet and nestled in her soft muff of raven curls.

His mouth went dry, and his cock twitched with anticipation. God's blood, but she tempted him to stay between her pale, satiny thighs and devour her. Spreading her labia with gentle fingers, he leaned in to sip her honey. Her swollen bud stood out, a tiny bit of flesh that quivered and elongated when he worried it with his teeth and tongue.

Her hot wet slit felt slick and slightly salty to his tongue. Saddle leather, horse hide and the damp, rich smell of the forest in springtime mingled in his nostrils with the erotic scent of aroused woman. Sounds of forest creatures and a gentle breeze rustling the leaves of the trees that curtained the clearing gave accompaniment to Jasmine's soft moans when he inserted two fingers in her cunt. Her juices flooded his hand and mouth.

More blood slammed into his cock. His balls tightened. Carefully, for he was so hard he barely dared to mount, he pulled away and heaved himself into the saddle.

"Free my cock, sweeting," he ordered even before he'd finished swinging her around to drape her legs across his rock-hard thighs.

Jasmine didn't hesitate. Her cunt wept, she wanted him in her so desperately. His braies posed little impediment but for the knot at the waist of his braies that didn't want to let go under her trembling fingers.

Finally it gave way. Cupping his heavy sac in one hand, she used the other to free his big, throbbing cock.

A sunbeam reflected off the gleaming ring, heightened the contrast between rigid gold metal and his purplish, swollen cockhead. He wept for her, too. A pearly drop of lubrication glistened in its dimpled eye.

He lifted her, impaled her inch by inch until she rested in the saddle. Her labia cradled his balls while her cunt eagerly took in the full length of his cock. She held onto his muscular shoulders, her gaze locked with his. Her entire being focused on the delicious sensation of fullness. The feelings coursed through her body one nerve to the next until she trembled with the intensity of them.

Jumbled feelings. Love for this strong knight who saved her from rape and certain death, took her in, and gave her pleasure beyond her wildest fantasies. Desire so intense that every time she clasped his cock within her body she wished she never had to let it go.

"Rajah..." Rolfe spoke softly to the horse in a strange, melodic language Jasmine had never heard before, and Rajah began to plod slowly along the path they'd taken moments earlier.

"Oh!" The horse's motion jostled them, just enough to heighten the delightful sensation of being filled beyond full with her lover's huge, hard cock. "Fuck me harder...yesss. I want to touch you." She burrowed beneath his tunic, seeking contact with warm, satiny skin.

"We could be seen along the road, sweeting." He glanced about, as though looking for their escort. "Even now my men may be close enough to see what we do."

Rajah picked up the pace, setting off vibrations that began where they were joined and radiated through her with every contact of the destrier's hooves upon the firm surface of the road. Even the thought of being observed heightened her erotic pleasure. "This feels so delicious, I care not." She tasted the firm, slightly salty sweat at the base of his neck and down the slit that left a tanned strip of his massive chest bare.

"Use your cunt like a fist. Yes. God yes. Squeeze me." Rolfe gasped, as though the effort it took to speak had stolen his breath. "I thank God I found you, sweeting. Oh, yes. Like that. Milk out my seed." He groaned, a loud, guttural sound that seemed to rumble from somewhere deep in his chest.

When his cock spasmed and began spurting his scalding seed deep inside her, the sensations triggered her own shuddering climax. Her quim clenched with every spasm. Shards of sensation spread, then burst in tiny explosions. Each explosion came stronger than the last, and they kept coming. More and more waves wracked her body until she slumped on his chest, limp and spent.

'Twas only when they came in sight of Hedgewick as the sun was setting that he lifted her off him and arranged their clothing. "We will sample yet another of life's pleasures in the privacy of my solar."

* * * * *

That night Rolfe noticed Jasmine's withdrawal. 'Twas almost as though her mind had fled, toward some place where he could not go. Though she'd bathed him and herself, she now stood, her luscious body still wrapped in a linen drying cloth, staring out an arrow slit into the darkness.

"Sweeting?" He hated times like this, when he couldn't reach her. "Do memories trouble you again this night?"

"Nay. 'Tis the lack of them that plague me. To have no past and no future—"

"Your future is here, with me." When Rolfe came near and enfolded her in his arms, he realized mere words would not convince her. "I love you, my Jasmine."

"Yet you cannot wed with me, for I have naught but myself to recommend me. Any children I give you will be bastards. I wish…"

Rolfe wished, as well. "I would wed with you. But you deserve more than a landless knight who holds this rotting pile of stone in his brother's name. Be assured that you hold my heart in your soft, talented hands. Forever."

A cool, damp wind gusted through the solar, making the candles flicker in their sconces. Jasmine shivered as she pulled the linen tighter around her shoulders.

"Sweeting, come to bed before you catch a chill." Rolfe shepherded her toward the big bed, wishing he could dispel her melancholy mood. "Will you pick a scene for us to re-enact this night?" he asked when she stopped by the window seat and stared down at the book that lay open there.

"Nay." Turning away, she went to the bed and crawled between the covers.

When he joined her, he found her curled up tightly like a babe, totally still but for the regular motion of her breathing. If only... If only she were the heiress he needed to secure his future. If only he had more to offer her and any children they might have.

He lay behind her for hours, until dawn's light began to filter through the arrow slits, stroking the gentle curve of her back as the breeze ruffled her raven locks. The faint tremors that flowed into his fingers infuriated him. By the bones of St. Jude, he'd help her find her past and keep her in his bed, against all who might come to challenge him.

"Marry me, Jasmine," he said, his words muffled against the silken strands of her hair. At that moment Rolfe cared not that she brought him no estates or title.

A great sob erupted, so deep it seemed to have come straight from her heart. "I cannot. For all I know I may be the meanest serf, unfit to bear your heirs...or, saints forbid, the wife of another."

"You came to me a virgin, love, a condition no serf who looks like you would be able to maintain for long around her masters. A state no sane husband would allow to continue longer past the saying of the vows than the time it took for the briefest of appearances at his own wedding feast."

"Sometimes I think I recall a gray stone castle upon a cliff overlooking the sea. Waves crashing against the rocky shore beneath it. The great hall had a hearth as wide as two men are tall." She paused. "I can make out no more. No faces but those that have haunted me before…"

Her words trailed off, as though she pondered possibilities too painful to put into words. "Rolfe, I lived in that castle…in my dreams I've seen myself standing at the bedside of some gravely injured knight. Heard my sire give orders to his men to take me away."

"Then you are no serf."

"Nay. I am…my name lies somewhere deep in my mind. I cannot…Yes. I see an old woman now. She calls me Demoiselle."

"'Tis the courtesy title given a maiden of noble birth. Think, sweeting. What is your name? The name of the castle in your memories?"

She turned in his arms, burrowing her face against the hard wall of his chest. "All I remember is an old woman helping me to dress, calling me Demoiselle."

A gray stone castle, on a cliff that overlooked the sea. Rolfe could think of only two within the distance of two days' travel that fit that description. He and Giles had overseen the destruction of one of them, in Lincolnshire, during their most recent service with King Henry. The other stronghold was to the north, about two days' hard ride away. Summerfield Castle lay near the oft disputed Scots border. 'Twas a fine castle as Rolfe recalled, held by Earl William, a marcher lord whose fury at the highlanders had apparently caused him to ally himself with some near neighbors who the king had outlawed and vowed to destroy.

"Might your sire be Earl William of Summerfield?" Rolfe asked gently.

Jasmine lifted her head and looked into his eyes. "I know not. Mayhap if you took me there...seeing it might stir my addled brain."

"Summerfield lies two days' hard journey from here, sweeting. I've glimpsed it only once, when Giles's army did King Henry's business in the North some months ago. It has two great circular towers and an older square one. The portcullis is emblazoned with a large, elaborate replica of a hawk on the wing. A deep moat protects the three sides facing land. The steep cliff protects it from intruders who would come by sea."

Her eyes tightly closed, Jasmine appeared to be trying to place the details Rolfe described—details he imagined only a warrior would recall.

"Does this place have a massive fireplace in the great hall?" Her dejected expression told him his description had opened no doors in her flawed memory.

Rolfe stroked Jasmine's silky cheek, hoping to dispel the anguish he heard in her voice. "I know not. We did not venture within its gates." The king had let his army bypass Summerfield. When he recalled the reason—that Henry had known Earl William lent succor to the northern robber barons they'd been fighting to destroy—Rolfe barely managed to hide the apprehension that washed over him.

"Jasmine, think on this. Did the sun rise or set over the sea?" Please God, her home would prove to be the keep in Lincolnshire, even though it now was naught but a pile of rubble and its lord had departed in disgrace for France.

She lay still for a moment, as if in deep thought. "The sun disappeared into the sea at eventide," she told him after a few moments' silence.

'Twas Summerfield from which she came. Bones of the Savior. Rolfe's emotions vacillated between joy and terror. His Jasmine was an heiress beyond any he'd have dared to seek. A marriage prize without equal if she was now her father's only heir. The heir of a man who stood on the cusp of disaster, if rumors that had circulated around the battlefield not two months past were true.

"Have you sisters, sweeting?"

"Nay. Only a brother. The one at whose bedside I stood vigil." She sounded strangely certain about that, as though that particular part of her lost memory had suddenly been restored.

Rolfe's hope dwindled, for he knew Earl William's only son had recently succumbed to his wounds. His credentials were such that he could aspire to win the well-dowered daughter of a powerful nobleman, but not the only heiress to a great estate. "I believe you are the demoiselle of Summerfield, sweeting. Too rich a prize for the fourth son of Comte deVere of Normandy, even though I enjoy King Henry's favor. He will wed you to a prince, mayhap even to one of his own sons." He'd not tell her he feared Henry's armies were even now laying siege to her father's castle.

"Nay!" she cried, rising from his arms and glaring down at him. "You have asked me to wed with you, and I now accept. I will have no other man in my bed. No other hard cock in my cunt, spewing its seed. Even now I may carry your babe," she said, her voice gentler now as she toyed with the rings in his tightening nipples. "Summon your priest and we'll say the vows, and then take me to this place you believe to be my home so I can regain the parts of me that I have lost."

"'Twould be dishonorable to wed you without your lord father's blessing, sweeting." Possibly fatal as well unless King Henry could be persuaded to order the marriage.

Jasmine clasped his face in her dainty hands. "If I knew who my sire was, 'twould dishonor him. But I do not know. You said you wished to marry me. If you still do, you will stand before the priest with me this day."

Rolfe wanted nothing more, but… "The banns…"

"…can be waived," she said. "The priest owes you his livelihood, so he will do your bidding."

"Rise, sweeting. We will break our fast, then depart for my lord brother's castle. If he agrees 'tis the right path to take, we will be married there ere we journey north to end the mystery that surrounds and confounds you."

A wife he loved who loved him, too? An estate even richer than his brother's? Rolfe allowed himself to fantasize as he and Jasmine rode there across Harrow's fields and meadows toward Giles' castle. He imagined himself a marcher lord, King Henry's faithful follower keeping order along the wild Scots border. He'd have strong sons and beautiful daughters. Jasmine would sleep in his arms each night, be at his side by day.

Not likely. Henry would most likely have his head for defiling such a marriage prize and give his woman to another more favored vassal.

Not while he yet breathed! With luck the king would remember the services he'd rendered…the fact that Giles had saved his life on the field of battle…the times they'd drunk ale and wenched and fought side by side for Henry's causes.

If they were very lucky, Henry might let him live and let this marriage stand, while confiscating Summerfield and bestowing it separately upon some other worthy knight. If so, Rolfe knew he'd have won the greater prize.

Chapter Six

"'Tis a bold move you plan, my brother. Marrying her could mean your fortune. Or your death."

His throat dry from the hurried ride from Hedgewick, Rolfe quaffed his ale, then met Giles's concerned gaze. "I wed with her for love. Not for the riches she may bring me."

"Nonetheless—your Jasmine is a great heiress indeed if she is Earl William's daughter. King Henry has declared the earl an outlaw and ordered his properties reverted to the Crown. We ride out on the morrow, to join his armies and take Summerfield by force."

"Why had you not sent me word?"

"Henry's messenger arrived only yesterday. Sir Tomas was about to ride out this morning as you rode through Harrow's gates to raise troops from Hedgewick and my other holdings."

Rolfe thought of Jasmine, her hopes of regaining her lost memory, and despaired as to what the coming battle might do to her fragile mental balance. "I would not tell her who we go to fight."

"'Twill be a difficult secret to keep, I think. Even now Brianna has likely told her your wedding celebration comes on the eve of a great battle."

*****

"There. You will wear this for your wedding." Lady Brianna pulled an undergown of shimmering gold silk from a coffer by the window. "I like it not on me, but with your vibrant coloring, it will be beautiful."

"Thank you." Jasmine doubted any garment would be less than fetching on the countess, whose unusually short blond curls framed a classically beautiful face. Even now, so soon after she'd given birth, her waist seemed small enough for her lord husband to span it with his two hands. "I will wear it gladly. I fear Hedgewick's attics provided little in the way of ladies' garb."

"It matters not. I was dragged to the altar to wed with Giles, wearing boys' clothes, with soot and tar smeared in my hair and on my face and hands. You see, I tried desperately to escape him. Now I thank the saints I did not."

The way Brianna's expression softened told Jasmine the match that had begun by force had become a love match. Having seen Lord Giles, who looked much like Rolfe only sterner, Jasmine had no problem imagining Brianna having fallen quickly in love.

"Is this the tunic you were seeking, my lady?"

Brianna took a practically transparent garment from the hands of a man—the biggest, most unusual-looking man Jasmine had ever seen. She tried without success to drag her gaze from his shining scalp, practically beardless face and...his naked chest and the colorful open vest he wore over ballooning pants. He reminded her of some of the erotic pictures in Rolfe's book.

"Thank you," Brianna murmured. "Jasmine, this is Arnaud. He is my right hand when my lord Giles must be about on the king's business. His services this night will be my gift to you and Rolfe. Go, Arnaud, tell my husband and brother the bride will be ready soon."

His services? Surely Arnaud could not be the eunuch of whom Rolfe had spoken... "This is too fine, my lady. I cannot—"

"Silence. You wed with my beloved brother-by-marriage. Naught is too fine a gift to celebrate his good fortune."

Confused, for she brought naught but herself to Rolfe, Jasmine stood silent while Brianna and two serving women fussed over her hair and fought over which of the fine girdles Rolfe had selected as her bride-gifts looked better with the shimmering sunburst of sarcinet and the gold undergown beneath it.

The picture book image of a woman and her lover, attended by a huge, exotic man who was not a man, made Jasmine wonder. The possibilities intrigued her. Did Arnaud pleasure Brianna when Lord Giles was off fighting the king's battles? Did he join the two of them to re-enact the scenes that had fascinated her so? She tried to control the lust that had her nipples tingling and her honey flowing slickly down her thigh, but the erotic images wouldn't go away.

"I think the rubies," Brianna said decisively, crisscrossing the long rope of gold chain interspersed with brilliant faceted stones. "We will sew you another gown that does justice to the sapphires and diamonds Rolfe also gave you as bride-gifts. Come, let us get you wed, so that you and my brother may enjoy the pleasures of the marriage bed for a few hours ere he rides out again on the king's business."

* * * * *

An heiress. The only surviving child of an outlawed earl he was bound to set out to fight on the morning after wedding her. A marriage prize too rich to aspire to, yet he was waiting here in Harrow's great hall in all his finery to take her before God and his lord brother's household.

Rolfe straightened the red velvet tabard that bore his family's device worked in gold thread and glittering gemstones. He adjusted the jeweled belt that held his dress sword in a jeweled scabbard. In his sweating hand he clutched the ruby-encrusted gold ring he'd soon place on Jasmine's small hand.

Perhaps if he fought valiantly and well, Henry would ignore the fact he'd wed the only living child of the Earl of Summerfield without royal consent, and let him live.

Mayhap, if he distracted himself with the activity around him, he could get his mind off the probable consequences of listening to his cock and his heart instead of his brain. He scanned the room, finding his two knights lifting their tankards with some of Giles's men while servants scurried about with food and drink they'd hurriedly prepared for a wedding feast.

And Giles, richly-garbed as befitted a belted earl in black velvet with the deVere device worked across his chest in diamonds and silver. He strode across the hall to join Rolfe. "They come now," Giles said, his gaze leading Rolfe's to the staircase that led to the Lord's Tower.

When Rolfe saw Jasmine his doubts fled. He'd do anything, risk anything, to keep this exquisite creature for his own. She wore her raven hair loose, crowned with a wreath of herbs and flowers, her golden gown belted with the ruby girdle he'd brought back from the East...and a knowing, very unvirginal smile lit her beautiful face when she saw him.

They made their vows and drank the toasts, broke bread and fed each other the tenderest morsels from the plate they shared. They laughed at the antics of traveling minstrels...danced...partook of the honey cake the cook had hurriedly prepared to celebrate their nuptials.

"We will prepare your bride for you, my brother," Brianna told Rolfe before spiriting Jasmine up the stairs.

Surprised, for he'd expected no bedding ceremony, Rolfe turned to Giles. "All know we anticipated our vows. I presented the bloodied sheet to your priest, as proof that Jasmine might already carry my son."

"The bedding is Brianna's gift to you. She lends you Arnaud this night."

Rolfe's cock swelled in his chausses. "Arnaud minds not?"

"Would you mind servicing a woman as fair as your bride?" Giles shook his head, as though Rolfe had taken leave of his senses.

"Nay." Tonight, his wedding night, seemed far removed from the villa Giles had captured near Constantinople. And he, very different from the frightened, injured boy his brother and the houris in the seraglio had tried to comfort after the death of his captors. "You showed me then that giving a woman pleasure could bring almost as great satisfaction as receiving it. I've not forgotten that day. Or the houri who let me lick her cunt and bring her to pleasure with a great glass dildo. 'Tis grateful I am that I use these lessons now to enhance the pleasures I bring my lady with my cock."

Giles laughed. "How does your Jasmine like the embellishments you wear in it?"

"She seems fond indeed of that jewelry. I thought perhaps to give her some of her own." The idea of putting his mark permanently on the parts of Jasmine that now belonged only to him made Rolfe's balls tighten and his cock grow stiff. "How long will it take for Arnaud to ready my lady?" he asked.

"I gave him the time it took me to finish a bottle of her father's finest wine and wash away the grime of battle from my body. Your bride, however, does not require the effort it took Arnaud to rid Brianna of the tar and soot she attempted to use as a disguise—and you need not a thorough scrubbing. We'll share another bottle of wine ere I take you to her."

* * * * *

Brianna and her ladies divested Jasmine of her bridal finery, folding it neatly and laying it atop the coffer of clothing and jewels Rolfe had brought from Hedgewick. She stood, her loose hair arranged to veil her nakedness, expecting at any moment for Rolfe to be propelled into the herb-laden bedchamber by his brother and those of the knights and men at arms who were sober enough to climb the steep, curved stairs.

Instead, Arnaud came in. And the ladies in waiting departed. "Arnaud will ready you for your husband." Brianna poured two goblets full of rich-smelling red wine and handed one to Jasmine. "His services this night are my gifts to you and Rolfe."

"Lie on the bed, my lady," the giant ordered, his voice soft yet rumbling, as if it came from deep in his barrel chest.

Jasmine hesitated. Though 'twas titillating to imagine being attended by two lovers, she was loath to violate a vow made before God. The priest's solemn words reverberated in her head.

...keep yourself only unto him, until death do you part.

"Go on, little sister. 'Tis no sacrilege. Arnaud, tell Rolfe's bride you mean him no dishonor. That your intent is to bring him greater pleasure on his wedding night. I leave you now. Rolfe will join you shortly."

The giant took a step toward her and clasped both of her hands. "Feel my hands, my lady. They are as soft and smooth as yours. I have no beard, no warrior's hard body. Most important to your lord husband, I have no cock or balls. My only road to pleasure is to bring satisfaction to my mistress." Exerting gentle pressure on her hands, he dragged them to his empty crotch. "Tonight it pleases her for me to pleasure you in the ways of the infidel. Lie down, and I will prepare you to accept Lord Rolfe's great sword."

Sexual excitement warred with fear. Jasmine lay near the edge of the bed upon a linen towel that had been left there. Velvet hangings at the foot of the bed obscured her view of the door. A breeze carried the sweet, musky scent from a hundred glowing candles—and a foreign, pungent but not altogether unpleasant smell—to her nostrils, making her fight to keep from sneezing.

That scent intensified when the giant eunuch sat beside her and began anointing her with a cool, thick substance. Her arms...calves...thighs...her cunt...

"What do you do?" she asked, alarmed at the tingling sensation that followed his touch.

"I make your skin smooth for your lord's pleasure, my lady Jasmine. While the paste works, I will pleasure you with these." He held up a stiff feather from a falcon's wing, a pair of ben-wei balls, and a string of large round pearls like the ones Rolfe had inserted in her cunt after their first mating.

Jasmine felt her honey begin to flow when Arnaud very gently spread her pussy lips and slipped the mercury-filled balls inside. Her arousal intensified with the motion he set off by laying his big hand on her belly and rotating it in a lazy circle. His other hand went to her anus, already sopping with her own juice, and she felt him inserting the pearls, one by one, past the tight opening and into her sensitive rear passage.

"Oh, yesss," she purred when he began stroking her slick, wet slit with the tip of the feather she'd seen. She lifted her hips, setting the balls in motion inside her cunt. 'Twas all she could do to suppress a scream.

Arnaud deserted her quim and turned his attention to her puckered nipples. "I need my husband now!"

"Not yet, my lady. I will remove the paste first." As though it pained him to do it, he withdrew the ben-wei balls, bending to lick the juices off her cunt before he lifted his head and began bathing her with a warm, wet sponge.

He had her so hot, she thought she'd die.

When he finished he slid the towel from beneath her, leaving her bare skin in contact with fine, soft sheets. Taking her hand, he brought it to her cunt. "Stroke your satiny channel. Feel how soft and smooth you are, my lady. 'Twill increase your pleasure, and Lord Rolfe's." He caught the end of the string of pearls in his hand and laid them in hers. "Withdraw them. Slowly. One at a time. 'Tis another means of giving pleasure to yourself when your lord must leave you on the king's business."

Impossibly, painfully aroused, Jasmine tugged gently, popping the pearls out of her body slowly, deliberately, as the eunuch instructed. She'd expected release, but her agitation only increased. She reached out for Arnaud even as she screamed for her husband, but he had moved out of her reach.

A creaking hinge and a sudden burst of a breeze hailed Rolfe's arrival. Not caring that his brother and a dozen drunken knights gawked at her unclothed body, Jasmine held out her arms to her magnificent, heavily aroused and equally naked husband whose jeweled cock rose proudly from its nest of soft dark hair. The ribald suggestions the men shouted at him served to make her honey flow more copiously, its journey down her slit made more erotic by the contact with her newly bared skin.

The door soon slammed, leaving her alone with Rolfe—and Brianna's giant eunuch.

"Your bride eagerly awaits you, my lord Rolfe," Arnaud said, his demeanor as calm as if he had not just touched every inch of Rolfe's wife's naked body, aroused her to such a fever pitch that she'd begged him for release. "Do you wish me to leave?"

"No. I wish for you to stay and help me give my lady pleasure. "'Tis her fantasy to be fucked by two men at once, and I'd see it fulfilled. Come, join us in my marriage bed and together we shall make her most erotic dreams come true."

Jasmine watched, aghast yet incredibly aroused, as the eunuch removed his garments and strapped a leather harness about his empty, hairless loins. A harness that held a beautiful blue blown-glass dildo—not large, as she assumed his own manhood must once have been—but well shaped and gently curving toward his slightly rounded belly.

While Arnaud readied himself, Rolfe sat cross-legged on the bed and stroked Jasmine's satiny channel, dipping two fingers into her sopping cunt and taking her slick, hot honey to his lips. Arnaud soon stretched out at her other side and began anointing her breasts and belly with oil made from precious herbs and spices.

Her own ragged breathing filled the silence, its pace and volume increasing along with Rolfe's as her lust blossomed, threatening to overtake her ere she could savor erotic sensations she'd experienced before only in her fantasies. "Fuck me now, my lord husband," she begged, her desire already at a fever pitch.

"In good time, sweeting. Spread yourself for me." Rolfe's voice sounded unsteady, as though passion had overcome him, too. He held himself still, though, the only motion in his body the pulsating of his mighty rod against her hip.

"I would pay proper homage to my lady," he told her when she'd done as he bid. Then he bent his head and took her in his mouth. The velvet stroke of his tongue on her labia drove her wild, and his hot breath bathed her channel and made her cunt weep to be filled with his throbbing cock that even now pulsated against her knee.

When Rolfe turned her to face him on her side, she went willingly, propping her leg behind his head to facilitate his access. She felt Arnaud's large hands spreading her arse, then circling her anus the way he had before inserting the pearls. Now, though, it wasn't a pearl he worked beyond that tough barrier but something larger. The false cock she'd watched him strap on. It was blunt, and slick with the same oil he'd used to anoint her tingling nipples.

She felt herself opening, like a rosebud, as the eunuch worked his dildo deeper into her rear passage while Rolfe kept tonguing her cunt. Arnaud's soft hands, so different from Rolfe's callused ones yet strangely sensual, massaged her breasts, making her nipples grow harder and longer.

Full. But not full enough. Jasmine wanted Rolfe's huge cock stuffing her cunt, his talented mouth suckling at her breasts...plundering her own mouth while he fucked her cunt and Arnaud pleasured her arse.

"My lord, I die," she said, whimpering at the sensual overload even as she wanted more. "Fuck me. Put your hard, hot cock in my cunt and help me find release."

He moved quickly, sliding up her body and filling her. As if they'd done it a hundred times before, he and Arnaud set up a rocking rhythm, stretching and filling her, then retreating only to fill her again. Sandwiched between their large bodies, she was bombarded from all sides with erotic sensations.

She felt full...stretched. The two cocks moving in and out, separated by the thin wall that separated her cunt and her arse, felt incredible. Her juices flowed, hot and slick, as one cock plunged in and the other withdrew. Ebb and flow...only the flow didn't stop.

Rolfe's mouth felt hot on her breasts that were already tingling from Arnaud's gentle touch. His teeth grazed her tender nipples as he latched on and began to suckle. The eunuch stroked the undercurve of her breasts while he settled his cool lips at the back of her neck and sucked at the sensitive spot just below her hairline.

Every cell in Jasmine's body threatened to explode. When Rolfe took her mouth and filled it with his tongue, plunging it in and out in tandem with the thrusts below, her cunt convulsed around him, capturing his cock and wringing out his seed while her arse clenched and shuddered around the false cock there. Rolfe was still spurting his hot life into her when the most intense climax of her life left her limp and exhausted.

* * * * *

"Never say I don't fulfill your every fantasy, sweeting," Rolfe told Jasmine the following morning. "I will miss you whilst we do King Henry's bidding."

The day had broken warm and dry. A gentle breeze caught a forelock of Rolfe's sable hair and tossed it back against his chain mail hood as they hurried across the bailey toward the horses. Jasmine brushed a speck of dust from the ruby-red silk tunic she wore over a gray linen undergown.

'Twas a perfect day but for the troubled look on her husband's face—and the implication inherent in the glittering plate armor he and what seemed to be an army of knights had donned atop chain mail. Sunlight reflected off polished shields and deadly tips of lances affixed to each destrier's heavy saddle.

She shuddered when she noticed the deadly-looking mace that hung from Rolfe's sword belt along with a broadsword in its tooled leather scabbard. Surely God would not have given him to her, only to take him away in battle. "What is this battle you go to join?" she asked as he set his helmet onto his head.

He raised the nasal and met her gaze. "'Tis King Henry's fight against the robber barons of the North. He bids us join the siege. Keep safe, my love. We will return ere long."

Jasmine tried to focus on Rolfe's parting words, but foremost in her mind over the coming weeks was a growing premonition that some ill would befall her bridegroom and she would be left adrift to bear his son—a woman without a past and without resources other than the charity of her husband's family.

* * * * *

Usually pristine streams that crisscrossed Summerfield ran red with blood, and bodies lay strewn across the bailey and in the great hall. Rolfe stood, his bloody sword still drawn, before a fireplace large enough to accommodate the reclining length of two large men. The fireplace Jasmine had recalled so vividly.

His bloodlust drained, leaving him breathing in the acrid, metallic smell of his enemies' lifeblood. He wondered how long 'twould be ere his own life would be forfeit.

"A fine prize this will be for one of King Henry's favorites," commented a knight from the army of one of the marcher lords. "A great estate and Earl William's buxom daughter. I warrant she'll be glad enough to be freed from her cloister."

Cloister? Had he wed with a Bride of Christ? "The earl sent his only daughter to a nunnery?" he asked, recalling Jasmine's dream—and her fear that she'd been a holy nun.

"Yes. Though I never met a lady less suited for the religious life. Earl William vowed to give her to the Church if God spared his heir, and when the boy rallied briefly, he packed Lady Joan off to a cloister in the Midlands. Useless, though. Young William succumbed to his injuries a fortnight after she was gone."

"Know you which convent?"

"St. Benedict's. The king has sent a troop of his men riding hell for leather, hoping to intervene ere she takes binding vows. It surprises me that you haven't heard—Henry ordered her taken to Harrow Castle to await his pleasure."

She's already there. Swelling with my seed. A messenger had brought that news to him and Giles a few days ago. "I had not heard."

Earl William lay at the top of the tower stair, a broadsword still clutched in his lifeless hands. Rolfe stared down at him, seeing instead his bride's fair face. How could this man have been so evil as to treat his own flesh as a human sacrifice? He wished his father by marriage yet lived so he might have the pleasure of skewering him.

"My lord?"

Rolfe looked up into the frightened eyes of a serving woman. "You need not fear. We do not harm women or children." He wiped his sword on his surcoat before returning it to its scabbard. "Are there more of you abovestairs?"

"A few. My lord, what will happen to us now that *he* is dead?"

"Your lady will return with her husband." The man King Henry chooses for her as soon as my body is as cold as that of her sire.

The woman's eyes widened. "But Earl William sent her to be a nun."

"That may be, but your lady is no nun." Despite his exhaustion, Rolfe felt his cock stir at the thought of Jasmine—Joan—and her definitely un-nunlike qualities in his bed. "Go now. Tell those who cower in fear that we will not hurt those who come in peace. There are dead who need a Christian burial."

* * * * *

"You what?" King Henry roared that evening, after the bodies had been removed from the hall and a fire burned brightly in the great fireplace of Summerfield.

"I married the woman I called Jasmine. I know her now to be Lady Joan, Earl William's daughter. Even now she quickens with my son."

His fists clenched, the king stared down at Rolfe. "Had you not fought valiantly for me, did I not owe my life to your lord brother, you would lie dead at my feet. As it is, you may forfeit your life soon enough. Tell me, how did you come upon this woman you call Jasmine?"

"On the way back to Hedgewick, which I hold in my lord brother's name, I heard a disturbance along the road. A band of brigands were about to ravish a lone woman when I dispatched them all to hell. When the woman regained consciousness, she knew nothing of who she was or from whence she came." Rolfe's knees hurt from kneeling on the cold stone floor, but he dared not ask to stand.

"So you kept her for your carnal games?" Henry's voice dripped sarcasm.

"Yes, sire."

"You did not think that she might have come from a cloister a few kilometers away from where you found her?"

"Nay. My lord, she wore no veil. Her hair hadn't been cut. And, no disrespect intended for I love my wife dearly, she acted like no nun I've ever encountered."

The king questioned Rolfe further, then bade him rise. "Can you tell me honestly you had no idea of your wife's true identity when you wed with her?"

"Nay. Though I wasn't certain until I saw yon fireplace that my lady had described, I suspected she might be the demoiselle of Summerfield. Though I knew I might be put to death for my audacity should that prove true, I loved her enough that I wished to wed with her and ensure our son's legitimacy."

Henry sat, motioning for Rolfe to join him on the settee. "I must think on this. On the one hand, I owe you as well as your brother gratitude for your strength in arms. On the other, you have made it difficult for me to reward a more worthy, stronger knight with Summerfield and its heiress while you yet live. How many years have you?" he asked, suddenly changing the subject.

"Four and twenty, sire."

"When did you earn your spurs?"

"Eight years ago. During the battle where my lord brother took a Welsh arrow meant for you."

"'Tis said you're a swordsman without equal. And that you are lethal with your lance. But I've heard naught of your ability to manage an estate or mete out judgment to those who serve you."

Rolfe took heart at the possibility that Henry was considering letting him live—not making Jasmine a widow ere she brought forth his son. "My lord brother will tell you I've whipped Hedgewick into shape. 'Twas a hotbed of rebellion, with its serfs an undisciplined lot, when Giles put me in command. I know 'tis naught compared with Harrow…"

"Or Summerfield," Henry commented. "The Scots continually harass the borders, and even now after I've restored order, the harsh life seems to foment disputes among the northern barons. I'd thought to replace Earl William with an older, more experienced knight."

The king raked Rolfe with a steely gaze. "Think you that you could control the North in my name?"

"Yes, sire."

"Then we shall test your mettle. My messengers will escort your lady home. I will call a tourney. If you defeat the challenges I warrant will be made by nearly every marcher lord, I will give you Summerfield—and your life. If you do not, I will give your widow to the man who defeats you."

Chapter Seven

"My ladies, a troop approaches. They bear King Henry's standard."

"Order the gates opened, and tell cook to prepare refreshment," Brianna told Arnaud.

He'd said they'd spied the king's banner. Not the silver deVere unicorn upon a field of black. Jasmine's throat tightened, and the small hairs on the back of her neck prickled as though they knew something was amiss. And she noticed that though Brianna smiled, she hugged her infant son closer to her breast as though she, too, feared the message they soon would hear.

"I bear greetings from your lord husband." The well-fed king's man handed Brianna a crumpled parchment. "I also bring word from King Henry. He orders that we escort the Lady Joan, whom you know as Jasmine, into his presence at Summerfield. We leave tomorrow at daybreak."

Joan? The name meant nothing to her, but her fingers suddenly felt icy cold though the weather was warm and sunny. "I beg you, sir, tell me my lord Rolfe has not suffered a grievous injury."

The messenger laughed. "Nay, the young rascal is unscathed. For now. He may not be so lucky when the king's tourney is done." He proceeded to explain the manner in which the king had chosen to deal with the problem of Rolfe having wed with her, without Henry's knowledge and consent.

"Rolfe is a fierce fighter," Brianna said, her tone soothing as she looked up from her embroidery. "He will prevail. According to my lord Giles, he won his considerable fortune in tourneys here and in Europe."

Brianna's words did little to allay the fear in Jasmine's heart then or later, while she packed the healing herbs she hoped Rolfe would not need. Bile rose in her throat, causing her to run for the garderobe as she'd been doing regularly for the past few weeks.

She could barely fathom that before Rolfe had rescued her, she'd apparently scaled a high wall and escaped from the Convent of St. Benedict three short days ere she'd have been forced to take her vows. Yet that was what the king's messenger said he'd learned from the prioress at the cloistered nunnery.

Now, because of her, Rolfe's life and fortune depended upon his skill at arms. Her future, as well, according to the messenger. The idea of wedding and bedding the knight who slayed her love brought up the rest of the meal she'd barely managed to choke down.

"Sir Rolfe will prevail, my lady. My mistress bids me to try and banish your anguish for a while." Arnaud's gentle hands warmed her heaving shoulders.

The human contact helped, but the only satisfaction her body sought now only Rolfe could provide. "Thank you, no. Tell the lady Brianna I wish to be alone tonight, to prepare for my journey and pray for my husband."

* * * * *

When three days later she saw the three towers of Summerfield in the distance, memories flooded Jasmine's mind. The battle…the dismembered body of her betrothed husband…her brother Will, grievously wounded and hovering near death. Her sire, turned madman sworn to wreak vengeance on the bastards who'd cost him his only son and heir. Her brother rallying, saying a few words...and her father ordering her sacrificed to a living death in the cloister of St. Benedict as thanks to God for having saved Will's life.

All was quiet, unlike the busy countryside she now remembered. The sun was sinking in the west, its orange glow lending a surrealistic glow to the dark gray stone walls. The castle gates loomed ahead, drawbridge lowered and portcullis raised, as though the king's party was expected and welcomed.

Strange. She recalled clearly that her sire had been no friend to Henry. Then she saw it. His putrefying body, hanging with a dozen others along the curtain wall.

Her bridegroom had left her to help slay her father and take his castle, but she wanted nothing more than to see Rolfe's beloved face, to lie with him and once more feel his great cock filling and stretching her cunt despite her queasy stomach and swelling belly. She'd longed for him for many anxious weeks...and she feared she'd grieve ere all was said and done.

Then he was there, and she was in his arms, and her pussy wept for joy. "I remember it all now," she murmured against the tanned, muscular column of his throat.

"Eleven knights have challenged you." Giles wore a worried frown when he entered Rolfe's tent on the tourney grounds a few minutes later. "The king has said he will allow no more." He named Rolfe's competitors one by one, and the two assessed strengths and weaknesses of each fighter while Jasmine—she could not yet think of herself as Joan—lay against Rolfe's muscular chest and tried to hide her fear.

She recognized some of the names, marcher lords who'd been loyal to the king. Baron deWilde and her odious cousin, Harold of Wye. The other names meant naught to her, though she recognized some surnames.

"Fear not, sweeting. I will vanquish them all."

Rolfe sounded confident, but she liked not the troubled look on his brother's face. From their earlier discussion she surmised that at least a few of the competitors had demonstrated great skill at arms.

"You must rest, my love." She stroked Rolfe's chest after Giles had returned to his own tent, then lay beside him when he stretched out on the narrow cot. "I am so sorry my insistence that we wed has brought us to this."

"I am not, for you are my destiny. I hope the journey did not overtire you." With infinite tenderness Rolfe stroked her silky cunt. "Tomorrow at this time we will celebrate my victory. Now stay beside me, for we both must gain strength from rest." After he extinguished the candle by their makeshift bed, he held her close.

He intended to sleep. But his cock did not. As Rolfe breathed in his Jasmine's sweet, erotic scent, felt her heart beating against his own, he had to have her.

"Open to me, sweeting." He slid his hands along her silky flesh, awakening her, torturing himself with the waiting...the need to claim his love once more. In answer to his whispered entreaty, she rolled over to face him and draped a firm thigh across his hip.

God's blood, but she was hot. Her cunt welcomed him with its honey when he slid his cock inside. It gripped him, milked him, made him want to stay forever—and burst into a thousand flames. 'Twas as if they were suspended in time, limited in motion on their narrow bed, locked together in lust and in love...

She drew his hand to her breast. "In a few months' time, my love, I will bear you a son. Does this please you?"

If tomorrow he died, something of him would live. Unless...he could not bear to think he wouldn't be there to hold his wife, protect the small life inside her. No, he had to survive, win the prize that would be his son's birthright.

He slid his hand between them, caressed her belly he now realized had become slightly convex since last he'd felt it. "I am delighted. 'Tis one more reason for me to defeat all challengers."

"I'm afraid."

"I will not lose. Cannot. Not when you give me so much to live for. Come now. Let me give you pleasure. Let me take my pleasure of my love. My only love."

In the darkness, with a breeze gently rocking the walls of the tent, Rolfe loved his Jasmine. Breast to chest, belly to belly, they lay together, moving slowly to the rhythm of the wind. The delicious friction of her cunt on his cock as they converged and retreated drove away the pride. The fear. Everything but the feeling of oneness with his love...his lover...his wife.

'Twas not too much later when he felt her clench his cock in uncontrolled spasms and caught her little cries between his lips. He came in long waves, gentle yet more intense than any he'd ever known. Waves that carried him over the edge and into a peaceful, strength-renewing slumber.

* * * * *

Sweat poured off Rolfe's brow when he brought Lucifer to a halt before the stand erected for King Henry and other noble observers. 'Twas hot, the sun beating down at noon. For five hours now Rolfe had taken on challengers and vanquished all but two. 'Twas as though love had made him invincible.

Smiling to hide her fear, Jasmine stood and draped another scarf over the end of his outstretched lance. "God go with you, my love."

"He tires."

Giles's words were barely audible but Jasmine heard. His whitened knuckles and tightly knotted fists said more than the words she was certain he meant no one to hear.

"He will prevail." God willing. Tense, she watched the next contender ride onto the field.

Giles took her hand. "Of course," he said in an obvious attempt to bolster her spirits. "Look, Rolfe has unseated him."

Jasmine's relief was short-lived, because unlike the others, this knight did not go down to his knees in surrender. Instead he drew his sword and beckoned for Rolfe to dismount and join him in swordplay.

"'Twill be all right, my lady," Giles said. "Rolfe will make short work of Lord Tibbets."

He did, but not until he'd taken what looked to be a painful cut through his chain mail chausses. Jasmine cried out when she saw he intended to remount and take on the last challenger, Baron deWilde.

Giles clamped a meaty hand over her mouth. "Do not. He needs not the distraction. DeWilde's a worthy opponent. Sit still and watch, or I will take you to wait in his tent."

Once, twice, three times the destriers charged. Three times lances hit shields, but neither knight fell. Lathered, sides heaving, the warhorses pawed at the chewed-up grass waiting for the signal to charge again.

DeWilde's lance made a glancing blow off Rolfe's shield. Jasmine screamed as he rocked in the saddle, his own lance dangling uselessly at his side. Oh, no. DeWilde turned his mount, rode at Rolfe again. This time when the lance rammed into his shield, Rolfe fell.

Jasmine's breath caught when she saw blood flowing down Rolfe's leg. Surely now he'd concede. She'd beg the king to spare his life, promise anything, even a lifetime of misery with the marcher lord who now stalked her love, his broadsword drawn.

"No. Do not die," she sobbed as Giles restrained her from running onto the field of honor. "I can give you up if I must, but I cannot bear it if you die."

"Rolfe will not die. He has too much to live for. Calm yourself. Look. Even now he rouses himself to fight."

Slowly, before her eyes, Rolfe stood on shaky legs and drew his sword. DeWilde came near, his shield protecting him while he hacked at Rolfe with ferocious wide arcs of his heavy blade. Then, as Jasmine thought all was lost, Rolfe dipped under his opponent's wild blows and slipped his sword between helmet and chain mail.

DeWilde went down, and Rolfe stumbled toward the dais, triumphant.

He sank to the bloody ground at the feet of Jasmine and his brother.

* * * * *

The fever lasted for days. The stench of rotting flesh made Jasmine gag, but she refused to leave Rolfe's side. 'Twas the evening of the third day since the tournament when he wakened and took her hand.

"You are mine," he whispered through hot, cracked lips. "Always."

"Yes."

Marnie, the old woman she'd seen in her mind, handed Jasmine more cool wet cloths to lay over the herbs she'd packed into the gash in Rolfe's upper thigh. "He will live," she said as she swabbed away the sweat that had pooled on his brow. "'Tis good the baron's lance missed his rod, lady. A fine rod indeed," she added, looking at the jewelry piercing it with a questioning gaze.

"Yes, it is." Jasmine could hardly wait until her husband, newly made Earl of Summerfield, grew strong enough to impale her on his fine, jeweled cock. "Kindly send word to his lord brother that Lord Rolfe has wakened."

"With pleasure, my lady Joan."

Rolfe lifted his head from the down pillow. "She may be Joan, but I am earl here and I call her Jasmine. My beautiful, fragrant flower from the East. My love and my life. Leave us now, that I may demonstrate how an earl seduces his countess."

A GIFT OF GOLD
ಐ

Chapter One
Summerfield Castle, Christmastide 1177
ꙮ

Set on a ridge overlooking the North Sea, Summerfield Castle's gray stone towers reflected the noonday sun, giving off a silvery glow. A welcoming glow indeed for the deVere men who shivered in their armor this December day. Earl Rolfe spurred his destrier, and soon he, Will and Gavin had outpaced the troop of knights and men-at-arms. The others could take their time, guard the wagons and siege engines they'd used to quell yet another rebellion in the midlands.

No doubt they all yearned for the comfort of home too...anticipated the pleasures that awaited them. Especially Gavin. For him this would be the last time he'd return to the castle where he was born and call it home.

As his father had done twenty-two years earlier, Gavin would wed with a great heiress and become master of her holdings. The wedding would take place ten days hence, at Summerfield, as part of the Christmas celebration. When he swung out of the saddle onto the ground of the frozen bailey, Gavin tried to tell himself 'twas time. That all would end well so long as he had land and titles to pass to his own son when he became a man. He even attempted to dredge up a bit of enthusiasm toward his betrothed, Lady Evelyn fitzSimmons, whom he'd soon meet for the first time.

A more sharp-tongued lady you'd be hard-pressed to find. Sends the servants a-runnin' for cover when something's not just right. Haughty, like nobody but her has more than a pisspot for a brain. She's a fondness for the table too...plump as a Christmas goose. Mayhaps barren. Mayhaps not although she gave her husband no bairns, for he was old and battle-worn. The words of the jongleur who supposedly had met the Lady Evelyn in her castle—soon to be his, Gavin reminded himself—sent another shiver clean to his balls as he dismounted and handed the reins of his snow-white destrier to a waiting serf.

That jongleur had also mentioned that Castle fitzSimmons, his betrothed's main holding, possessed high round towers. Three of them. If he found his bride too repulsive, he could confine her to one of them as soon as he got an heir on her. The way Gavin felt today after three long months of fighting, he'd have no trouble dredging up the necessary enthusiasm to fuck any female on two legs, no matter how distasteful she might prove to be.

When they passed over the drawbridge, Gavin noted a lighter-than-usual number of men-at-arms along the wall and wondered briefly which of their northern neighbors might be causing havoc along the border. No matter. Had it been a serious problem that required dealing with, a messenger would have galloped to their train to enlist their aid.

'Twas past time for him to enjoy the comforts of home, the gaiety of the season. Putting his worries out of his mind, Gavin mounted the stone stairs and made for the great hall, with Will and their lord father at his heels. Mayhap he and Will would share a wench or two, as had been their habit for seven years now.

Gavin recalled that first encounter, when they'd first learned some things were more fun when shared. The accommodating milkmaid they'd encountered in the barn at Harrow ere going to the castle to enjoy their fourteenth birthday celebration had apparently thought so too, despite the clumsiness of two boys with no finesse and no staying power. At least she'd come back for more. Many times over. By the time they'd finished their fostering, the sassy little whore had given them as much training in pleasuring women as Uncle Giles had provided in the use of weapons and strategy for battle.

Back home, they'd honed the art of seduction, learned it added to the excitement when they added toys and erotic games into the mix. Gavin's cock stirred when he recalled the way one adventuresome kitchen maid had creamed herself when they stripped her naked and tied her to the cross-shaped beam they kept in their chamber to hang their plate armor. They took her in tandem, Will's cock in her cunt and his in her tight, hot ass, while she whimpered and moaned and begged for more.

Excitement hung in the air. Proud of his battle-hardened physique, Gavin flexed his muscles against the warm steel rings of his chain mail. He reckoned there was some of the boy left in him, for he yearned for home and family, merriment and the sorts of ribald amusements that always made his lady mother shake her head. Debauchery ran ever rampant at Summerfield Castle, but especially during the Christmas season. His cock grew harder as he anticipated dipping it into the sweet, hot cunts of one or two willing wenches.

The hall smelled of precious spices and roasting meat. A huge fire crackled in the fireplace that would soon hold the massive Yule log they'd cut last spring. Flickering beeswax candles cast shadows on walls bleached to a grayish white, illuminating tapestries that bespoke the triumphs and tragedies the earls of Summerfield had seen over the years. Gavin would never tire of hearing the tales depicted in scenes of the Holy Land—settings his father had described. Exotic places Lord Rolfe had seen when serving as his brother's squire on the crusade that nearly cost him his life. Gavin inhaled deeply, took in the heady fragrance of the spruce boughs and pomander balls that decorated the hall.

"Jasmine!" Lord Rolfe shouted from the base of the winding stair to the north tower. Gavin knew his father had gained politically by wedding with his mother, but 'twas obvious to all that the countess had fired his sire's blood. Damn, from the hot, needy look he saw in his father's eyes, Gavin doubted not that the fire still burned, hardly banked at all in the twenty-two years since they'd wed.

Lady Jasmine ran down the stairs, flinging herself into his father's arms as soon as he'd laid his helm and gauntlets on a long, narrow table by the stairs. Lord Rolfe lifted her, swung her around in circles. "'Tis good to be home once more. You told me not of any trouble along Summerfield's borders in your last message, my love."

"Reivers. Clan MacFarlane from the look of their plaids, said the serf who brought the news. I sent a party out to chase them back over the border." Lady Jasmine laid a hand on Lord Rolfe's mail-clad chest.

Gavin would have liked naught better than running the wily Scots laird through with his broadsword and consigning him to hell for all the trouble he caused—but damn! Not now. His ass ached from the long ride, his throat was parched for lack of ale. He stank of the road, his saddle and his destrier. He turned to his twin, resigned to riding out again, postponing the start of the yuletide celebration. "Shall we ride out and join in the rout?"

"It will not require us both. I'll go, be sure the bastards are running, tails 'tween their legs," Will said. "After all, 'tis my inheritance they plunder. Besides, you've got a wedding to prepare for."

Summerfield. His brother's legacy. Not Gavin's. And his upcoming wedding to a widow he'd not laid eyes on. Not very cheering thoughts though they all were true. "If you do not mind, I'll stay. My arse is saddle-weary, and you're right. My sword won't be needed to vanquish no more than a few bloodthirsty clansmen. I'm for a bath, some wine and a warm wench—not necessarily in that order."

* * * * *

The lord's solar smelled of fresh evergreens and precious incense brought at great cost from the East. Earl Rolfe deVere lay back in his tub later that evening, sipping mulled wine whilst his lady wife rubbed away the grime of battle from his naked body.

"'Tis good we will all be together this holy season," Lady Jasmine murmured, her soft hands stroking Rolfe's chest before reaching under the water and squeezing his fast-awakening cock. 'Twas a miracle that after twenty-two years, his lady still could arouse him with the simplest of touches. "I want you to name Gavin Lord of Misrule."

The younger of their twin sons held a special spot in Jasmine's heart—his too. Still Rolfe had to laugh. "That honor should go to one of the serfs, sweeting."

"'Twill be the only way Gavin will ever rule Summerfield."

"I know. And I'm aware the law of primogeniture rankles you. But take heart. Gavin surely won't have to earn his way by hiring out his sword. I've already gifted him with a king's ransom in gold and jewels, he's betrothed to the fitzSimmons heiress and I'm certain he'll win more titles and estates by force of arms, as Giles and I both have. Even now he and Will plan a fierce campaign against Laird MacFarlane, and I expect that one day soon they'll rout the clansmen clear back to the highlands from whence they came. They'd best, ere that wily Scot makes off with all my livestock. When they do, I shall ask Henry to grant the

MacFarlane lands to Gavin, though I know not whether he will. 'Twould make the deVere family among the most powerful in all England."

Jasmine frowned as she worked the soap into a lather and scrubbed away some stubborn dirt from Rolfe's forearms. "Tell me about this prisoner Will sent word that he is bringing back."

"According to his message, some men-at-arms who were patrolling our northern border caught her on Summerfield land. A Scots lass wearing the MacFarlane plaid. I'd nay be surprised were it Laird MacFarlane's own daughter. A wild lass from all I hear. If it be she, her presence should liven the Christmas festivities. Especially for our sons who are ever searching for another pretty wench to seduce."

"Speaking of seduction, I have missed you." Jasmine's touch lightened to a caress, and though she stroked his arms, it was his cock that stiffened and throbbed. "Does your bath water grow cold?" she asked when a tremor of pure desire shot through his flesh.

"Nay. But I grow hot." Rising, Rolfe took a length of linen and began to dry himself. "Get you to bed, my lady, that I may drink of your sweet honey. 'Tis too long I've been away."

He'd never get enough of her, not if he lived a hundred years. His beautiful countess who'd brought him wealth and title, and most of all the love of a lifetime. "Have you a picture you'd like for us to re-enact this night?" He gestured toward the beautifully illustrated pillow book that had fascinated her from the moment he'd shown it to her years ago.

"Tonight I wish for you to take me as though you're starved. As though you've been without a woman since last we fucked." She lay back, her raven hair spread across the snowy bed linens, her legs spread and her cunt glistening in the light from the fire.

"Who's to say I am not starved, my beautiful lady? 'Tis true," he added when she shot him a skeptical look. "When I think of you, it destroys any passion that might rise in me for the camp followers who service my men."

Her smile warmed his heart, set his balls on fire. "I too have starved, my lord earl."

"Then let us feast together." Tossing aside the drying cloth, Rolfe joined Jasmine on their massive bed and straddled her, offering his cock for her to feast upon as he buried his face between her shapely thighs.

Her whimpers and the copious flow of hot, sweet juices from her cunt attested to her need—a need Rolfe was determined to slake as he flailed her clit with his tongue. When she closed her lips around him, his cock swelled to near bursting against the heavy ring in its head, and his nipples tightened against the small gold rings that had adorned them for nearly thirty years. The tiny sounds she made as she suckled him made this encounter incredibly erotic...incredibly arousing.

Tonight he felt not one moment older than he had when he'd first taken the maiden he called Jasmine to his bed, nor one bit less grateful that God had sent him a fallen angel without a memory to tutor in all the arts of love. Her clit hardened and swelled when he tongued her there, and when he slid a finger into her cunt and found her wet and ready, he had to caution himself to make the moment last.

She felt tight. So tight he'd not have believed she'd borne him four sturdy sons if he'd not watched each of them emerge from her slender body. And God's bones but her cunt fit his cock like a glove, hot and slippery and schooled over the years in pleasure with the ben-wa balls she wore each day as she directed the castle servants.

Her anus drew his attention, made him remember their wedding night—and the eunuch Arnaud who had initiated that part of his bride's lush body to the pleasures of the flesh. Mayhaps—nay, though Arnaud would be arriving with Giles, Brianna and their children to celebrate Gavin's marriage, Rolfe had not been able to curb his possessive streak sufficiently to ask again for the use of the big, docile creature who'd guarded his sister-in-law's virtue since her marriage to his elder brother.

With gentle fingers Rolfe invaded Jasmine's rear passage as he used his tongue to fuck her cunt. When she stopped stroking his ass cheeks and slid her hands between them to cup his tight, aching balls, he could waste no more time on the niceties of arousing her. If he did not take her now, he knew he'd fill her mouth with burst after burst of his pent-up seed.

"Stop, my Jasmine," he ground out, turning and positioning his cock at the dripping entrance to her cunt. "I'd come inside you, where my seed may yet take root."

"You'd still give me a daughter, would you not?" Her smoky eyes shining, Jasmine framed his face in her hands as she lifted her hips to meet his initial thrust. "'Tis to my shame that we've not been blessed again."

"Hush. I told you, sweeting, ere we were wed, that deVere men throw sons. 'Tis not your fault we've not been blessed with a tiny lass. And I'd as soon not risk you again in the effort."

"What will be, will be. Oh my love, you fill me so completely. How I've missed you, missed this." She gasped when he sank into her to his balls, finding along the way that spot that always produced an instant climax. He braced himself for the hard, quick contractions of her spasming flesh, held steady as she came then started to thrust again.

He'd make her come for him again. This time he stroked the silken flesh of her throat, her beautiful breasts. Sucked upon the nipples that had fed his sons. He murmured words of sex and love and the lasting devotion with which she'd blessed him over the years.

When she screamed again with the force of the pleasure he gave her, he let go of his iron control and buried his cock deep. So deep he could hardly feel where he ended and she began as he spurted out his seed deep within his Jasmine's beautiful beloved body.

"On the morrow, I'll name Gavin Lord of Misrule," he told her later as they lay spoonlike beneath the soft, warm sable furs that made their blanket. "I cannot deny my Jasmine anything her heart desires—except her little girl. And a love match for the son of her heart."

* * * * *

A love match. Lady Evelyn fitzSimmons paced her tower room at Summerfield, coveting the painfully obvious mutual emotions she'd seen passing between her betrothed husband's handsome parents.

Not that she'd seen them from any less distance than she'd glimpsed Sir Gavin, soon to become her bridegroom. Upon her arrival at Summerfield yesterday, she'd begged Lady Jasmine not to reveal her presence, to allow her to remain in the guest tower alone to contemplate her upcoming wedding. Evelyn glanced down at her ample curves and tried not to envy her future mother-in-law's lithe, slender body.

No way could she, with her love for good food and fine wine, starve off enough flesh in five short days to compare with Lady Jasmine...not that she'd do it if she could. Not even for Sir Gavin, with his great height, powerful body and a face that would do justice to a dark angel. Evelyn reminded herself her betrothed was wedding with her for her estates, not because he loved her or even desired her person.

She shouldn't mind that. After all, she'd wed with the elderly and bellicose Baron fitzSimmons four years earlier for the wealth and position he'd offered. As she'd done then, her betrothed could always visualize the land and castles that came with her if looking at her made him regret his decision.

But what if Gavin couldn't stomach the thought of bedding her? Unlike women, men had to summon a measure of passion ere they could perform in the marriage bed. While she'd found some, like her late husband, who'd appreciated her ample curves, she'd come across a good many potential suitors who'd run at the thought of bedding a woman whose waist they couldn't span with their two hands. Handsome, virile men like the one she was about to wed.

You're naught but the veriest coward, Evelyn. Otherwise you'd not be cowering in the shadows, keeping your presence secret from Sir Gavin and the castle folk. Though she chided herself for a fool, Evelyn had stayed glued to the peephole in the tower's thick stone wall, afraid to face her betrothed and mayhaps see revulsion spreading across his angel face.

"My lady?" The maid set a brimming tray of food on the table by the single window.

Obviously Cook had gotten word from someone — probably the serving girls who'd been setting the high table when Evelyn had arrived — of her generous proportions and assumed she possessed a healthy appetite. By Evelyn's quick calculation, the wench had brought enough meat, cheese, bread and wine to serve the entire high table. She fought down feelings of resentment that had naught to do with the slender maid who'd inadvertently caused those sour emotions to surface.

Evelyn made herself smile at the housemaid who apparently intended to stay and help her ready herself for bed. "What's your name, girl?"

"Mavis, m'lady. I'd help you with yer clothes if I may, so's I can answer m'lord Gavin's summons. He doesn't like having to wait." The wench's knowing grin hinted her purpose with Evelyn's intended would be more pleasurable than merely assisting him at his bath.

An idea began to form. What if... "Mavis, do you think I might take your place? My lord Gavin knows me not. I'd—"

"Fuck 'im, m'lady? For that's what he's summoned me to do. He's asked for two though. I suppose ye could disguise yerself and take Henny's place."

"Two?" She'd heard of the debauchery that went on with the young lords and knights at Summerfield, but she'd not believed until now that it went so far. Still...the idea of deceiving Gavin intrigued her. 'Twas a way, though a dangerous one, to learn whether he found her curves appealing—or appalling. "I'll do it, but I want him to believe I'm a servant girl."

It would serve her satyr of a future husband right to fuck her, not knowing he'd be doing it nightly soon enough. And he wouldn't be able to help feeling at least a bit abashed once he learned the real identity of the strange woman he'd plowed just days before taking marriage vows with her.

Mavis gave her a critical once-over. "Ye'll need clothes. And ye'd better not talk like the fine lady you are. Wait. I'll borrow a gown from Cook. She be about yer size."

Her ego stung a bit by Mavis' last remark, Evelyn stripped down to her plain white linen shift. Excitement won out over the sense of uneasiness that lingered in the back of her mind. "By God, I'll test out the bonny lad I'm weddin' and he'll be none the wiser."

While Evelyn twirled about, getting into the role of a wanton serving girl and testing the manner of speaking she'd use, Mavis returned with a drab blue garment.

It smelled like grease from the cooking fire and felt like grit against skin used to velvets and satin. Evelyn wrinkled her nose in disgust. Her disguise had better work to make wearing this rag worthwhile.

As they went downstairs, crossed the great hall and ascended a steep curving stairway to another of Summerville's crenellated towers, Evelyn silently laughed at the prospect of putting one over on her lascivious future husband.

"Let's tell him yer name's Evie, m'lady. Yer name be pretty, but it'd never belong to a serving wench."

Evelyn laughed out loud. "Fine. Evie it is, but ye'd best not be callin' me m'lady unless ye want to spoil his surprise."

Chapter Two

In the north tower, Sir Gavin paced naked across the cold stone floor. Where were the wenches he'd summoned to come relieve him? Damn it, he'd had this raging hard-on since leaving his Uncle Giles' castle a week earlier. Shivering, he tossed another log onto the fireplace grate. The warmth slowly curled around him, almost like his absent lovers should be doing in yonder bed.

Gavin's stone-hard cock twitched, reminding him of the wenches. He'd demanded a pair out of habit, even though he doubted Will would return in time to join in the fun. Gavin considered inviting his other brothers, eleven-year-old Alfred and thirteen-year-old Henry, who'd come home from fostering for the holidays, to take part in the debauchery, but he quickly discarded that idea. His lady mother would box his ears, much like she'd boxed them years ago when he and Will had enticed two serf girls to their beds to celebrate their twelfth birthday with some mutual bodily explorations. As he recalled, the whipping he'd been administered had caused far more pain to his ass than the wenches had provided him in pleasure.

Oh well, he was hard enough to service them both and ask for more. Where were they anyhow?

"M'lord?" The dark-eyed girl who suddenly appeared in the open doorway to the solar was young and pretty. Mavis, if he recalled her name correctly from their last encounter. Though Mavis was eminently fuckable, it was her companion who made Gavin's heart beat faster. Her flaxen hair flowed loose to her generous hips, and her ripe breasts heaved—whether with anticipation or fear, he could not say.

Plump as a Christmas goose, she was. Anxious to get on with the fucking too, if her haste to cast off the filthy servant's gown was an indication of her ardor, and not merely a perfectly understandable desire to be free from the pervasive smell of roasting meat that clung to the ugly garment.

It mattered not if she weren't already slick and wet. She'd get hot for him soon enough. He'd stay by the fire, keep his ass warm while the chill air made his lovers' nipples pucker and drew goose bumps on their naked skin. "Both of you. Disrobe and come to me."

He imagined the one wench's pale hair wrapped around his cock, warming his balls. Trailing over his thighs and ass while she sucked him dry…while he tongue-fucked the tiny brunette and introduced her to a cock she'd not yet seen. The ruby-red blown glass dildo had caused almost as much of a furor among the jades at King Henry's court as his and Will's distinctively pierced rods.

First he wanted to sample the plump wench's quivering breasts. They'd more than fill his large hands, and their rosy puckered nipples tempted him mightily when she lifted off her shift. He longed to swirl his tongue over a small blood-red birthmark he spied just below the nipple of her left breast. Rising, he smiled at her when her huge china-blue eyes opened wide and her mouth formed a sensual "O" at the sight of his pierced, heavily jeweled cock.

"Gawd, somebody whacked off yer foreskin and stuck pins through yer knob!"

"You didn't know? There's hardly a soul on the marches who's not heard of the deVere cocks. Come, take a closer look." Ere dawn broke, the buxom beauty would have examined in minute detail the rod that apparently caused her such consternation. Gavin's balls tightened painfully as he looked at her soft, soft skin. The saucy twin moons of her well-padded ass. He cursed the pale gold curtain of hair that hid her features while she knelt and took his seed sac in her dainty hands, even as he longed to bury his face in the fragrant, silky strands.

"Must be a king's fortune just in this big gold ring." Lubrication seeped from his slit when she rotated the heavy ring that pierced his cockhead, and when she tugged gently on one of the gold studs that ringed his corona, he moaned. God's blood, but she had a magic touch. "Mavis, ye didn't tell me we'd be fuckin' a prick full of precious metals."

It suddenly struck Gavin that he couldn't recall having seen this angel who was quickly setting his blood a-boiling. He wouldn't have missed her if she'd been about the castle while he was home. Ever mindful as he was of the earl's enemies using whatever means they could to get at members of his family, Gavin asked sharply, "What's your name, girl?" Though her speech marked her a villein, he didn't often see a serf so obviously well-fed. Or one with such soft, velvety hands and shining hair.

She stood, met his gaze with a degree of self-possession unusual in a servant. "Evie, m'lord. I come from the village."

"Well, Evie, you've a sassy mouth. I suggest you use it to pleasure me." Ironic, this smart-mouthed woman bore a variation of the same Christian name as Lady Evelyn fitzSimmons, his betrothed. "Come closer, Mavis. I'd pleasure you too."

Evie's pale hair formed a gleaming blanket about her upper body when she knelt again at Gavin's feet and took his cockhead between her soft, moist lips. The silky strands brushed his thighs and tickled the tender flesh of his scrotum while he fondled Mavis's small, pert breasts.

'Twas all Evelyn could do to resist chomping her betrothed's huge, jeweled sword. Be damned if she'd share him with the serving girls once she was his wife!

"Ah, Mavis, my sweet. You taste as good as ever!"

"'Tis always a treat whenever you call me, m'lord Gavin."

"You, Evie girl. Take a bit more of my cock. Suck it harder, would you?"

She'd suck him harder, all right. She opened wider, lowered her mouth on him until the ring in the end of his cockhead tickled her throat. And deliberately let her teeth graze the bejeweled ridge of his corona.

"Ow. Easy there, or you'll bite it off."

If only...but no, 'twas her own pleasure tool she'd be destroying if she followed the impish voice inside her head. Her tool. On their wedding night she'd lock it away...and set it free only when she wanted satisfaction!

Still it rankled. It was Mavis getting the benefit of *her* betrothed husband's hands and mouth. Mavis whose passion he was arousing whilst she, Evie, set his own blood a-boiling. Deliberately she dug her nails into the muscular flesh of his buttocks as she sucked his cock with feigned enthusiasm.

"Ah, Will, I assume you routed the MacFarlane clansmen ere they paupered us all. Come on, join in the fun."

God in heaven, Lord William must have just walked in on them. Evelyn dug her nails in harder, clamped her lips down harder on Gavin's swollen cock. Unsure whether to flee—not likely possible, she imagined—or stay and take part in a fuckfest that involved not only her betrothed but his older twin brother, she hesitated.

A moment too long, it appeared, for she felt chilled skin against her back and a pair of cold hands plucking at her nipples. Hot, sweet breath prickled the skin on the sensitive nape of her neck as soon as another pair of hands—Gavin's hands—swept her hair over her shoulder.

"Who is this delectable wench?" Like Gavin's, Will's voice was deep and sensual, the voice of a skilled lover. When he nibbled at her exposed earlobe, he made her shiver.

"Here, Will. Meet Evie. She'll warm you quickly enough, I'll warrant. Oh yes, Evie girl. Suck me dry. Make me forget that ere a sennight passes I'll be a married man."

A married man who'd ne'er again fuck a serving girl. Evelyn redoubled her efforts as Gavin's brother tugged her nipples and nudged her weeping cunt with his own fine blade. How would Gavin feel when he learned he'd given his bride to his own brother?

'Twas an arousing thought...an arousing situation. God's blood, how hers boiled when Gavin tossed the furs from the bed onto the floor, lay down before the fire and drew her lips back to his cock—while Will spread her legs and knelt behind her, rubbing his pulsating sword along her wet slit, in the creases where her thighs and body met. She wanted to rear back, take his cock into her body when it nudged the dripping entrance to her cunt...the sensitive tissue around her anus.

Vaguely Evelyn's mind registered that Mavis sat squarely on Gavin's face and that he was using his tongue to lap the servant's well-used cunt while tugging Evelyn's own nipples between his calloused thumbs and forefingers. The delicious sensation of fullness dispelled any jealousy...anger. For she had them both. Her betrothed and his brother. The slightly salty taste of the slick juices that seeped around the ring in Gavin's cock tickled her tongue while his brother's love tool primed her quim, spread her honey along her slit, over the puckered entrance to her rear passage.

The sensual assault made her crazy with wanting more. Wanting them both. Evelyn's excitement bubbled as she imagined how 'twould feel…one identical twin's cock plowing her cunt, the other invading her ass. "Ohhhh," she murmured around the turgid flesh stretching her lips when something hard and cold slid past the weeping lips of her quim and lodged in her cunt. Not a cock…what?

Whatever it was it heated quickly, set her cunt afire when she contracted her inner muscles around the smooth, hard object. It slid in and out, stoking the flames, making her suck harder on the cock in her mouth as though that would entice the other cock to fill her empty, aching ass. The virgin hole Mavis had warned her to prepare. To stretch as she'd once stretched her cunt for Baron fitzSimmons whose tool had been whispered to be immense.

The glass phallus she'd used was a puny toy compared with the throbbing cock that now pulsated in her mouth.

Anticipation built as Gavin used his rough, calloused hands to pinch her nipples, tug on them. Gavin rocked back and forth, making her take his cock deeper down her throat with each leisurely thrust. She swallowed, wanting more of that long, hot shaft while she kneaded his seed sac ever so gently, feeling the twin orbs within shift against her seeking fingers.

Lord William's hot cock between her thighs probed her puckered rear passage. Slippery with her own honey, it sought entrance. Will's calloused palms rasped against her tender flesh as he squeezed her buttocks, spreading the plump, moist cheeks for his cock.

"You want her cunt or her ass, Gavin?" he asked as though offering the breast or a leg of a roast duck on his trencher. "Our father tells me you're Lord of Misrule, so you rightfully deserve first choice."

"I want her cunt." Gavin's reply was barely audible since he didn't bother to move his mouth away from Mavis's slit. Apparently Will heard it though. Before Evelyn had time to think, he'd positioned his cock and pushed until its jeweled head popped past the tight muscle and seated itself within her ass.

Ohhhh. It hurt, yet she wanted more. Wanted Will's big cock to fill her there, her betrothed's to replace the slender object that barely filled her cunt.

Slowly. When Will buried himself deeper, the throbbing heat seared her ass. Her moans reverberated around Gavin's cock that stuffed her mouth. Sensation flooded her, made her tremble at the dual invasion even as her quim wept for more.

"Come take her cunt," Will said. "I warrant it's as tight and welcoming as her ass."

Evelyn heard a slap of flesh on flesh, and a whining protest from Mavis. Then Gavin laughed. "Up with you, Mavis. Go play with yourself whilst I fuck Mistress Evie. You may choose one of the toys from yonder box."

Every one of his bulging muscles, each inch of his golden hairless skin set Evelyn's nerve endings on fire when Gavin slid beneath her. His steaming shaft seared her belly, her mound, the tight little love button that begged for attention. Another hand—Will's, she thought—reached under her belly and retrieved the dildo from her cunt. When Will raised her, he thrust forward, burying his cock to the balls in her ass. His seed sac wedged between her ass cheeks.

It hurt. But it felt good too. The burning, stretching sensation. The incredible heat that overtook her when Gavin's jeweled cockhead sought and found her quim, slid home.

God's blood but she'd never felt so full. So taken. The brothers' two big cocks impaled her, stretching her. Throbbing within her body, the tandem motions bounced off the thin wall of tissue that separated them. "Ohhh, melords," she whimpered, barely remembering in her passion to disguise her speech—recalling just in time that she played the role of a wanton serf girl.

"Like this, do you?" Gavin asked, flexing his hips and sliding in her cunt up to his balls while his brother slid out of her rear. God's blood. They fucked in perfect harmony. Delicious, hot sensations bubbled in her cunt. Gavin's hands kneaded her breasts, tugged at her nipples. He nipped the soft flesh at her throat, took it in his mouth and suckled. Tongued it as if to soothe the bruise he made with his teeth and lips.

The dual assault was too much. The pleasure too great. Pressure built with each rocking thrust, each brush of Gavin's hard ridged abdomen against her soft, rounded belly, every nudge of Will's against her ass cheeks. Gavin's scratchy cheek abraded her throat, her jaw. Every hard pinch of his fingers on her distended nipples dragged her closer to ecstasy. When they increased the pace, rocking her harder between their bodies and ramming their big cocks deeper into her quivering holes, she came in long, exhausting bursts.

Starbursts, blue, red, gold, purple, exploded in her head as the two cocks spasmed within her body, spurting wave after wave of steaming seed into her cunt. Her ass.

The heat of her orgasm mellowed into a warm glow when they lay back, one on either side of her, each holding her as though they'd not easily let her go.

Evelyn would have liked to sleep in the brothers' identical strong arms but she dared not. Untangling herself from their embraces, she admired their big hard bodies whilst she put on her gown then gave out a sigh as she and Mavis took their leave.

'Twas God's own pity she couldn't wed them both.

Chapter Three

'Twas the first day of Christmas. Wine flowed and all manner of sweetmeats and pies accompanied the usual bread and cheese with which the occupants of Summerfield Castle broke their fast. Two burly men-at-arms turned a spit on which a whole deer was being roasted for the coming feast. More men tended the hearths in the kitchen, where Cook presided over the preparation of the traditional boar's head, more mincemeat pies and several swans whose roasted carcasses would be refeathered ere the evening meal began.

Named Lord of Misrule by his parents before the hunt where he'd personally skewered that unfortunate boar, Gavin lost no time once they'd returned to the hall in leading the Yuletide merriment. His first order was for his twin to bestow kisses on every lady and wench caught breakfasting in the great hall.

He laughed when Will returned to the high table, his cock tenting his tunic. "Methinks you lingered too long with the MacFarlane wench, brother. Remember her sire, and that the acorn falls not far from the tree. She's as likely to skewer you as suck your cock." Gavin leaned back in his lord father's high-backed chair and considered what mischief he'd order next.

Will laughed at the warning. "Never fear, my misguided Lord of Misrule. I'll guard my back. And my cock. Where is the plump pigeon we sandwich fucked yestereve?"

Gavin wondered that himself, until he remembered. "She said she came from the village. Mayhaps I'll visit her there ere I order the firing of the Yule log. Nay. I want not to wait that long to fuck her again." He spied the other wench, and bellowed, "Mavis! Come you to me."

The wench bowed low, giving both twins a fine view of her pert, ripe breasts. Gavin took her hand, bid her rise. "Fetch Evie to me. She stole away yestereve while we two dozed. Off with you. I'd see her ere we go to drag in the Yule log."

His lady mother shot him a look that needed no translation. She was not happy that he'd publicly singled out one of the castle sluts. She'd be less thrilled if he ordered another one to service him before one and all. When she turned back to his father, though, Gavin decided another order might serve him well. "As Lord of Misrule, I order the Earl and Countess of Summerfield to retire to their bedchamber. Methinks they need more rest this Christmas Day."

His father laughed then stood and took Lady Jasmine's hand. "We thank you, my Lord of Misrule. I've been away too many wintry nights, and I long to pass this day with none but my lady. My people, I wish you all a Happy Christmas. We will take our leave, and join you again ere the feasting begins—with permission of Gavin, Lord of Misrule."

After waving his parents away, Gavin set the assembled knights and ladies to dancing and singing familiar carols while he waited impatiently for Evie. His time for play could end at any moment—would necessarily end with the arrival of his betrothed. While he didn't expect to care particularly for her, he'd not insult her by dallying with a peasant wench before her aristocratic nose. 'Struth, he held out a shred of hope that in Lady Evelyn he'd find the sort of love his uncle Giles had discovered with the stranger he'd been ordered by King Henry to wed.

Still, Gavin intended to make the most of his remaining freedom.

* * * * *

"Sir Gavin said you're to come to him now, m'lady. He be Lord of Misrule and ye dare not disobey." Mavis wrung her hands. Apparently the idea that she'd be punished if she couldn't produce "Evie" petrified her.

"Surely he'd not cause you harm." Though Evelyn had heard tales of debauchery that she now knew firsthand were true, she doubted Gavin would resort to violence against those who served them—Lord of Misrule or not. "'Tis impossible that I masquerade before the entire gathering of revelers as a serving wench."

"If we dressed ye in Cook's gown—"

"Think, girl. That disguise does nothing to change my face. All who see me will know who I am if they've ever laid eyes on me before. Those who haven't will figure out quickly enough who Sir Gavin's bed wench was when I appear as myself to say my marriage vows." Though she'd not been to King Henry's court, Evelyn had hardly been a recluse. Chances were good—excellent—that at least one of the knights and ladies celebrating Christmas and the upcoming wedding at Summerfield would recognize her no matter how she tried to disguise herself.

"God's teeth. 'Twill cause a furor of gossip. What have I done?"

Mavis scrunched up her forehead as if she were in deep thought. Finally she spoke. "Mayhaps ye should ask for yer betrothed husband to join ye here. Confess yer deception. It's for sure he's hot to fuck ye, so he might forgive ye."

And Gavin's destrier just might grow wings and fly. But Evelyn could come up with no less odious solution, however hard she tried. She began rifling through the trunk that held her wedding finery. When she found a sheer white silk gown and forest-green velvet tunic, she thrust it into the maid's trembling hands. "All right. I cannot see any alternative, though I expect he will want to throttle me. Help me dress, and then go tell Sir Gavin that the wench Evie wishes him to meet her in this tower."

"Evie wouldn't meet him dressed fit to kill, m'lady," Mavis said, a dubious expression on her face as she looked at the luxurious fabric. "She'd meet him in somethin' she knew would stiffen his rod right quick."

From Evelyn's observation of yestereve, she deduced that it took very little to make her future husband's cock stand at attention. She wasn't certain, however, that she wanted it randy and ready this morn. Mayhaps...but no. She needed to greet him with dignity, explain away her actions of the night before.

Bones of Saint Aegis, what had she done? While there was a small chance Gavin would accept her having disguised herself to meet him and learn if he desired her, only the veriest idiot would stand for her having fucked not only him but also his twin brother while she played the role of wanton wench.

"It matters not. My only hope is that he will want my properties enough to wed with me ere he slaughters me the way you say he did the boar on this morning's hunt." Evelyn snatched the garments from Mavis's hands and yanked them over her head. "Hurry, sew the sleeves on and lace the tunic. As tightly as you can."

Why should she care how she looked? 'Twas certain Gavin would not. Still Evelyn sucked in her breath while Mavis laced the sides of the tunic, holding her arms out of the way. Knowing it to be her best feature, she left her hair uncovered, brushing the pale strands until they shone before catching it up within a jeweled snood.

"Go, Mavis. Summon my Lord of Misrule ere I lose my courage and jump from yonder window."

Chapter Four

ಐ

"M'lord of Misrule, the lady Evie begs ye meet her in the guest tower."

Saucy wench. Dared to defy the Lord of Misrule. Gavin's cock twitched. It ever liked a challenge. "Rise, Mavis, and take me wherever it is that Evie cowers. I'll not take my displeasure out on the messenger." He glanced about the hall. "Will, I cede you the duty of dragging in the Yule log. I'll return to light it ere long."

"You need not my help in taming Evie, brother?"

"Nay. We may enjoy her later, once I've tied her to my bed where she belongs."

* * * * *

The thought that Evie had been fucking with one of his parents' noble guests irked Gavin as he followed Mavis up the winding stairs. Why, he didn't know, because 'twas obvious she was naught but a castle whore. He noticed when they reached the solar door that Evie was occupying the space he imagined his lady mother had ordered saved for the guest of honor—his bride.

And that Mavis was rapping respectfully on the closed door and waiting for permission to enter.

What the...was that Evie? In silk and velvet, her ample tits practically spilling from the low neckline of the gown. Jewels in rainbow hues glittered from the gold mesh snood that barely contained her pale tresses. The buxom whore must have lost her mind, pilfering the finery of one of his parents' guests. God's nightgown, but she looked good enough to eat, cleaned up and wearing something other than that greasy servant's gown. She looked better wearing nothing at all.

Quickly he stepped inside the door, slamming it in Mavis' worried-looking face and throwing the bolt. No need to get a guest involved in Evie's punishment. He'd relish doing it himself. Mayhaps he'd even take her to the Great Hall, order the revelers to pay her homage as they would a great lady—as they would his bride. Strip her naked and fuck her in broad daylight, before the assembled knights and men-at-arms.

Gavin opened his mouth to speak, but naught came out. Evie held him speechless. Enthralled. Mayhaps he'd take her with him when he left here, buy her raiment like this and lock her away in a tower at Castle fitzSimmons for his pleasure alone. Once he'd done his duty and gotten an heir on his bride, he amended when his conscience tweaked him.

"You dare to steal our guests' raiment?" he asked when he found his voice.

"'Tis mine. I am Lady Evelyn, your betrothed wife."

"You lie. You're Evie, a castle whore who pleasured me and my brother yestereve. You could be flogged for being here, you know. Take off that purloined finery, lay it carefully upon yon chest and service your Lord of Misrule. I may yet let you go unpunished. Or I may not."

Her pale eyes flashed fury—or was it fear? "I tell you, I'm Lady Evelyn fitzSimmons, soon to be your bride. Do I sound like some peasant wench?"

She sounded not like the jade he and Will had fucked until she fainted from the pleasure of it. Today her Norman French sounded fit enough even for King Henry's court. And her tone as haughty as the jongleur had described. But 'twas impossible. No lady would have... "Disrobe or I shall rip the garments off your ripe, trembling body."

She made no move to obey, and that infuriated him. He stepped closer, so close he felt her heat, her fear, and laid a hand just below the crest of her left tit. "If I find the mark of Satan on this ample breast, I'll know for certain that you lie."

"Nay, you will not. You will know your bride came to you, wishing to learn if she could summon your lust. Evie and Evelyn are one and the same."

As though he'd been scalded, he jerked back his hand. "The marriage is off," he snapped, ashamed that even now his cock rose to salute the jaded bitch his sire had contracted for him to wed. "I'd not breed my heirs upon the veriest of whores."

"Who are you to name me whore? Think you I'm any more anxious to be plowed by a whoremaster who calls for not one but two peasant wenches to slake his lust on his arrival home before he even breaks bread and slakes his thirst for wine?"

"You risk your safety, Madame. Enlighten me. For what earthly reason did you decide to play my whore when in a few short days you'd have become my bride? To fuck not only me but also my brother?"

"I'd heard...that you were a cocksman of some repute. I wanted not to wed with you if," she paused, as though reluctant to go on, "if you could not dredge up the desire necessary for you to do your marital duty with me."

"You heard I sometimes couldn't stiffen my rod for a lover?" Gavin searched his memory but couldn't recall ever having suffered that malady.

"Nay. But I lost two suitors my guardian brought to me...two who said they'd not abide a fat, pale pigeon in their beds. I wanted to be sure you were not—"

"Well, you found out. Madame, your appearance does not disgust me, but your actions of yestereve certainly do. By the Rood, you allowed my brother to fuck your ass while you sucked my cock. While I plowed your cunt and filled you with my seed." God's nightshirt! The memory of her cunt milking his cock as he climaxed deep inside her was as vivid as if it were happening now. He might have gotten her with child already. He'd never even thought of pulling out, the way he always did with the wenches he fucked.

His sire had threatened to disown him and Will if their seed took root in the bellies of any Summerfield villeins. He could only imagine the punishment that would result from him impregnating a lady and leaving her unwed. "The marriage is back on," he spat out, the expression on his handsome face anything but happy. "You may already carry my heir."

"What if I do not wish to wed with a whoremaster who likes to share his women with his brother and God knows who else?"

"'Tis not your choice. I will tell the priest you carry my child and you'll not be able to refuse to say the vows."

The flat, unemotional delivery of his edict told Evelyn more than words could have that Gavin planned further punishment. Punishment she deserved, without a doubt, yet he deserved it too. After all, 'twas he who'd called for two whores to pleasure him. He who'd invited Lord William to come join in the fun. It was he who'd moved on her and in her in perfect tandem with his twin. Such perfectly coordinated fucking was not a skill learned in one or two encounters unless her guess was seriously off.

"Will you share me with your brother after we are wed?" she asked ere she could hold back the words.

His smile belied the chill in his voice. "You liked it, didn't you? Me in your cunt, Will in your ass? Stuffing you like the Christmas goose now roasting in Cook's oven for tonight's feast? You ask if I'll share you again once we're wed? I may, since you've proven it creams your cunt so well. I'd not wish to deny you your bawdy pleasures. Will and I have ever shared—our training, our knighting...'tis natural that we've shared our wenches too. I see no reason now to stop."

"'Tis against God's laws."

"So is fucking. That doesn't mean fucking isn't done every day, every hour, by everyone from the King to the lowest of serfs. Evie, I know you like it. Like it well indeed. You came so hard I thought you'd scream the castle down when Will and I were tandem fucking you. I am glad to find you have blood as hot as mine. Mind your mouth, or I'll confine you to a tower—and confine my fucking to a willing mistress or two, once we settle in at Castle fitzSimmons. And do not ever think of cuckolding me. The only fucking you'll be doing in future is with me—and Will, if he visits and I wish to share."

Gavin obviously thought he held the upper hand—in truth, he did. Still Evelyn couldn't resist pointing out again that as she had sinned, so had her betrothed.

His dark eyes flashed fire. "You are fortunate 'twas I and not my brother who took your cunt, for you're not high enough in the king's favor to be given to a future earl. I'll hear no more whining about my actions, now or ever. Come, there is no reason for you to hide in the tower. And I'm too angry with you to fuck you now. Partner me in the revelry, but remember, I demand your obedience in all things."

Thinking acquiescence the better part of valor, Evelyn meekly followed her angry betrothed down the stairs.

'Twould be time later to test her seductive skills—learn whether they were sufficient to persuade Gavin that having sex felt better than exacting retribution.

* * * * *

By the time the Lord of Misrule returned to the hall and introduced his betrothed to the assembled crowd, the roe deer had been hauled from the fire and taken to the kitchen for further preparation. The twelve-foot-long Yule log they'd cut last spring lay near the door, ready to be dragged to the huge fireplace and lit with the charred remains of last year's log. Laughing, Gavin led the knights and men-at-arms in the annual ritual, lighting the crackling heartwood kindling in remnants of the cooking fire. He touched the blazing kindling to dry bark on the huge log, lighting it instantly.

The instant igniting of the log foretold good luck for the household, just as eating the first offered mince pie was said to prevent bad things happening in the coming year to the one who ate it. Evelyn munched a flaky pie Gavin had given her, saying a silent prayer that the superstition was true. If it was, Gavin would forgive her...and their marriage would be one of joy and contentment.

"Let the merriment begin. I command you all to celebrate Christ's birth—and the crowning of the Conqueror a hundred and eleven years ago this day." Gavin lifted his goblet, downing its contents in a single swallow.

Thankfully, Lord William's attention focused on a red-haired, skinny wench wearing what Evelyn thought looked like the MacFarlane plaid. Strange. She'd heard Summerfield warred with Clan MacFarlane over some dispute or other. "Who is that woman with your brother?" she asked Gavin when he returned to her side.

"Lady Margaret MacFarlane. She is my lord father's guest—or should I say hostage? Our men-at-arms caught her on Summerfield lands yestereve, and Will brought her here. Though his intention was to hold her as surety for her wily father's good behavior, it looks as though he's decided to use her for another purpose."

Evelyn didn't doubt that, for Will had his hand in the Scots maid's bodice, feeling her skinny tits in full view of anyone who looked. He bent, whispered something in her ear, smiling at her reply. He squeezed her shoulders then strode toward Evelyn and Gavin.

"I beg your aid, Lord of Misrule. I'd have you order Lady Margaret to bathe me."

"Consider it done." Gavin slammed his goblet on the heavy oak table, drawing the attention of most of the revelers. "Mistress Margaret MacFarlane, I command you to go now and bathe my lord brother Will. I expect him to smell as fresh as the flowers from our mother's rose garden ere you're done."

Margaret blushed prettily. Evelyn envied her that, for when embarrassed, her own cheeks turned fiery hot and her pale skin mottled most unattractively.

Gavin lowered his voice, to where only those close by could hear. "Fuck her for me too, my brother. Unfortunately I must stay and order the merrymaking." He gestured toward Evelyn, the action insulting. "And, of course, entertain my dear betrothed. I assume you notice the resemblance between her and the buxom whore we pleasured yestereve."

Will had the grace to lower his gaze. Oh no. Here it came. The heat, the blotches and splotches. Knowing her cheeks and chin were fast becoming a hideous mass of red and purple welts, she was determined not to let her embarrassment show further. "Sir Gavin is too kind. Few of my suitors have ever likened me to a favored whore."

Gavin's furious look satisfied her that she'd managed to get under his skin.

Chapter Five

As Gavin and probably his wanton future wife well knew, Will couldn't care less about the bath he'd requested that Lady Margaret MacFarlane give him. When they arrived in his room, though, a steaming tub awaited them. His cock twitched when he remembered how sweetly the Scots wench had fitted against his chest, belly and groin on the ride back to Summerfield last night. All day he'd wooed the lass. Now he savored the prospect of bedding her.

Damn it, she'd made his cock rise to attention, his ballocks tighten in their sac the moment he'd found her struggling against the hold of two of Summerfield's men-at-arms. Though at first she'd refused to identify herself, she'd obviously been no serving wench, for her garments had been much too fine. Now she stood before him, sleeves carefully removed from the white linen gown she wore beneath her plaid, young but ripe, rosy-cheeked and possessed of eyes the color of a stormy sea. Reddish-brown hair framed her face in a riot of curls. When she bent to pick up soap from the stool by the tub, her dark green MacFarlane plaid gaped, providing him an arousing view of the upper curve of small, firm breasts.

His cock rose in salute. God's teeth, but he wanted to fuck her, now. He cared not if she'd spoken true when she said she was Laird MacFarlane's daughter. Whoever she was, she was his prisoner, ripe for plundering. His guest. Surety for the laird's good behavior if he cared about her.

He'd not been able to drag his gaze off the pretty maid from the moment he dragged her into his saddle and brought her home. The glint in her eyes when she looked at him was distinctly lascivious.

She eyed him that way now as she stood in his bedchamber while he disrobed. Her velvety pink tongue darted out of her mouth as though she wanted to taste him.

"I would have you bathe me first. Then I shall take my pleasure of you."

"Honor demands you protect my maidenhead."

Will didn't feel it necessary to point out that there were many ways for man and woman to pleasure each other that did not involve stealing a maid's virginity. If Lady Margaret still possessed it — which he doubted from the way she stared at the prominent bulge in his chausses as though she could barely wait to feel his cock piercing the channel between her long, slender legs.

Sir William deVere was the most beautiful man she'd ever seen. Tall, powerful-looking, with golden skin and hair the color of a raven's wing. His eyes, so dark they looked almost black, sparkled with good humor — and something more. In silvered chain mail, with a tunic of black and gold slung over his broad shoulder, and in the black chausses and simple tabard he'd just removed, he'd made her quim quiver. Just looking upon him now, watching his hard chest muscles ripple beneath that tawny sun-kissed skin while he untied the cross-garters that held up his braies, had her juices drizzling from the edges of the iron maiden she wore and down her inner thighs.

That he was one of a matched pair seemed too good to be true.

Lust practically stole Margaret's reason when Will shot another dazzling smile her way. Did he wear jewels in his shaft, the way 'twas rumored the earl did? She imagined the big knight's cock pierced with glittering gold adornments much like the baubles she wore in her ears and quim. She'd find out soon enough what he looked like naked.

As she moved closer to him and the huge oaken tub, the dangling clasp to her girdle swung back and forth against her mound, clinking melodically against her chastity belt and setting off a fierce need in her belly. One that would nay be satisfied as long as she wore the damned device. In truth, her maidenhead would be inviolate as long as the key remained securely locked in her sire's strongbox at the seat of Clan MacFarlane. As long as they held her here as surety for her father's continued good behavior.

Still, Sir William could ease the aching in her breasts, the weeping of her cunt. And she had ways she could relieve his lust for as long as he held her hostage.

A willing prisoner she'd be, if she could entice Sir William into her lonely bed. No woman should have lost three betrothed husbands on the field of honor, or reached the ripe age of nineteen as yet unwed and unbedded, locked in a chastity belt to preserve her value as a marriage prize. She dropped down in a curtsy she knew provided him with a good view of her breasts, a glimpse of the pink areolas that ringed her aching nipples. "My lord, may I help divest you of the rest of your clothing?"

"'Rise, that I may see you. And you may see me."

No woman could resist him when he curled those sensual lips into a smile. Nor when he held out a calloused, well-shaped hand to ease her up from her curtsy. When his gaze settled on her breasts, 'twas as though he'd seared them with fire.

He bent, lifting his loose black shirt over his head. When she took it from him, she smelled the scent of woman. Another woman. Jealousy bubbled up in her, but when she saw how the muscles in his glistening hairless chest rippled, she cared not that he'd slaked his lust on someone else since he'd held her in his arms on the long ride to Summerfield Castle yestereve. "I will remove the rest. I wish to sink into yonder tub ere the water cools."

The bulge of his sex caught and held her attention as it grew to massive proportions within his black knit chausses. She could not drag her gaze away.

"Like what you see, my lady? My sword salutes your beauty. And protests my own neglect of its special needs during battle and on my journey home."

"You are—very large." And she was very wet and becoming wetter by the moment.

His laughing eyes mocked her, made her nipples tighten and tingle within her gown. "'Tis a benefit in battle, my lady."

"I mean…" Sudden heat scalded her cheeks, and knowing her embarrassment must be evident turned her skin even hotter, "your—"

"Cock? Ballocks? Do not tell me a lady whose eyes look upon them with such obvious interest cannot say the words?"

His amused look annoyed her. By the Lady she'd not let him intimidate her. She met and held his gaze. "Cock. Ballocks. They seem unusually large."

"The better to give you pleasure when we fuck, sweeting. Come, remove the last of my garments and you may see how hot and ready you've made me. Then I would have you join me in my tub."

She knelt, loosed the cross-garters that held his braies to hard-muscled, shapely calves. Then, slowly, she skimmed her fingers up the outsides of his rock-hard thighs…over narrow hips. Full of anticipation for what she'd discover, Margaret hooked her thumbs into the fabric on each side of his waist and tugged the stretchy material down.

His cock sprang free, long, thick and throbbing, curling gently upward toward his navel. The rumors about the lords of Summerfield apparently were true, for Sir William's huge, throbbing rod had no foreskin. It bore a thick gold bar that passed horizontally through its purplish, plumlike head. A row of glistening gold balls winked all around the prominent corona, inviting her gaze, her touch. A pearly drop of lubrication had already gathered in the slit at its tip.

Margaret's mouth watered with the need to taste that tempting liquid, to run her tongue along the long, thick column of his shaft and trace its distended, pulsating veins. His large pink seed sac made a luscious velvety cushion for the four pairs of ruby studs that marched down its center, and her fingers itched to caress that softness, to feel the cool, smooth surface of the cabochon rubies in each end of the thick bar. "'Tis a beautiful cock, indeed." Leaning forward, intent on licking away that intriguing droplet of moisture, she couldn't resist asking, "Why do you embellish it so?"

"I am glad I please you, sweeting. As for the jewels, Gavin and I were each given a unique piercing as babes, and we chose to emulate our sire as we grew to manhood. An infidel prince had ordered him circumcised and pierced when he was captured as a youth." He paused, lifting his stiff rod by the bar that passed through its head. "I was circumcised and pierced here, and a small bar was placed through my cock soon after our birth, so all might distinguish me from Gavin, who was pierced in the same way as our lord father. The bars were changed frequently for thicker, longer ones as I grew. Once I achieved manhood, I added additional jewels."

"Do the piercings not hurt you?"

"Nay. They cause no pain once the wounds have healed."

"Your brother and father are pierced differently?"

He held up his rod again, indicating that intriguing slit in its very tip. "They wear a captive ring that passes through this slit and exits on the underside of their cocks, just in front of the corona."

In truth, Margaret liked the glittering look of Will's mighty sword. "Do the piercings enhance…?"

"The jewelry is said to make lovers' pleasure more intense. I can only vouch for the fact that it heightens my own sensations." His hand on her head urged her forward, as though he wanted her to take him in her mouth. Then he pulled back. "Come, I would bathe first. Disrobe for me."

"I should not…" But his hot gaze scalded her, compelled her to loosen her golden girdle and lift off her plaid and the plain woolen gown beneath it. She stood in her shift, shivering not so much from the chill of the room as from her reluctance for him to see her shame—the prison far more confining than the luxuriously appointed solar here at Summerfield Castle where he'd ordered her to be held under guard.

"I would see you. All of you." He stood in the tub, water lapping about his muscular calves. His huge cock saluted her, rearing up from his hairless groin toward the ridged muscles of his belly. Its golden studs glowed in the candlelight, held her gaze. "Disrobe. Now, ere the water cools."

Perhaps since he removed his own pubic curls, he'd not mind that her own quim was bare as a babe's, its fiery bush having been removed before her old nursemaid had fitted the rigid gold device between her stinging labia and locked the belt securely about her hips. Slowly, listening for his reaction, she lifted her shift, baring herself to the big knight's lusty gaze.

"You too are pierced." His harsh intake of breath could have meant he liked what he saw...or that he did not. Only when she tossed away her garment and looked into his obsidian eyes did she know for certain. Sir William apparently welcomed a challenge—the challenge presented by the glittering gold device her father had ordered locked about her waist ere sending her to be captured by the powerful Earl of Summerfield. And the dangling clit ring that served as extra security against randy would-be lovers.

"'Twill ensure you nay return with a deVere bastard in your belly, girl," he'd said when she protested. Margaret was none too certain that was true when she saw the glint in Will's dark eyes.

Will chuckled. "I've yet to find an iron maiden that can defeat me, sweeting. Come, let us play in the bath."

"And if I do not wish to join you, my lord?" she asked as she stepped closer to his tub.

He smiled, showing her straight white teeth and an inviting rose-pink tongue she could practically feel lapping at her pebbled nipples. "Then you must pay a forfeit. Know you not the rules of the game?"

"What would you have of me? I possess naught but myself, not even an extra plaid to protect me from the chill in the night air."

"I wish a gift of gold." His gaze settled between her legs, upon the golden ring that pierced her love button and held it out from a small round hole in the gold shield. "Perhaps I will take the one that pierces your tempting clit."

She moved to the tub and stepped onto the wooden stair, then paused so he could see. "'Tis welded shut, my lord. If you want it, you must tear away my flesh as well."

Smiling, he slipped a finger through the dangling ring, tweaking the hard little nub and making more of her hot, slick honey slither down her thighs. "That would be a tragedy, my little one, to hurt such precious flesh as this. I could always summon my lord father's armorer and have him break the weld. But I know many ways to give you pleasure. Ways that do not require that I remove this pretty ornament or the cruel device it helps to hold in place. We shall explore them all."

"But your pleasure, my lord? Would you let me satisfy you with my hands?"

He reached farther between her legs and ringed her puckered rear entrance with a calloused fingertip. "You possess two other holes as well as your soft, gentle hands. I plan to make good use of them all. Come, join me. Help me scrub away the stench of the hunt."

As she stepped into the water she laughed, a tinkling, merry sound that went not with her stern Christian name.

"I shall call you Meggie, for Margaret's much too serious sounding for one as sensual as you." God, but she made his cock stand at attention as few maidens could, his tastes having been jaded by serving girls who asked for naught but a quick fuck. Will stroked between her firm, silky legs, over the warm gold shield that left her pierced clit and puckered rear entrance unprotected, while it guarded the entrance to her sweet cunt.

Her soft moan at his touch had his balls drawing up, tightening in their sac. With one finger he delved beneath the iron maiden and felt the base of a rigid metal plug that stretched and filled her cunt as only a man's cock or tongue should do. "What is this?"

"'Twas my sire's idea when he commissioned the device from the goldsmith in Edinburgh. To ready me for a man, he said."

Will had always thought Laird MacFarlane a madman and thoroughly agreed with his lord father's assessment that the man bore careful watching and would benefit from being skewered at the tip of some Summerfield steel. He couldn't deny, though, that this particular one of the wily Scot's ideas showed a certain fiendish cleverness. To restrain his daughter from fucking yet keep her hot and wet with the very device that prevented a lover from filling her cunt with himself, while incredibly cruel, had required intelligent thought. Such a device had possibilities in the torture chamber. Still, he could not imagine a father forcing such a cruel device on his own flesh and blood. "How long—"

"Three years. Since he caught me pleasuring myself one dreary winter day. Twenty-eight days since the ring you seem to like so well was inserted, ensuring that no man can easily remove the device even if he should manage to break the lock."

A tempting proposition, to break that lock and take her fully! He'd do it, but first he'd teach her all the other pleasures he anticipated. Will rotated the clit ring, felt the weld that sealed it. The hole in the shield was too small to slide the ring through. Perhaps he could cut off the shield…

Mayhaps he'd let it stay. Bring her and himself to climax without penetrating her tight glory hole. At least for now.

Her sweet cream oozed from around the slender finger of gold, soaking his finger, perfuming the solar with the heady musk of man and woman and mutual arousal. Needing to taste her, he sank into the water, sitting cross-legged, the tip of his throbbing cock bobbing on the surface. "Spread your legs for me, Meggie. I would slake my hunger."

She stood, her feet planted on either side of his straining hips, her satiny labia held open by the chastity belt. The ring in her clit swung back and forth, tantalizing him, tempting his tongue. Her firm inner thighs glistened with her fragrant juices, juices that smelled like woman, slightly salty and a little bit sweet, with a hint of some precious perfume from the East.

Will lapped her up, all the time toying with the clit ring and the tiny, rock-hard bundle of nerves it pierced. Gently he took that sensitive flesh into his mouth and suckled it, swirling his tongue around it then spearing it through the ring and tugging it beyond his lips, into the hot recesses of his mouth. God's teeth, but she inflamed him. His balls throbbed painfully, as though they would burst if he didn't gain release.

With his hands, he stroked her, coaxing out more of the tiny whimpers and moans that began deep in her chest and made their way slowly out of her mouth and into his ears. She tasted like heaven and hell, and suddenly he wanted nothing more than to rip off the cruel device she wore and fuck her until they both fainted from the pleasure.

Instead he wet his fingers with her sweet honey and ran them around the puckered entrance to her ass. One finger slipped inside, then two. She tensed at what he guessed might have been an unfamiliar touch, then sighed. Her muscles relaxed, letting him sink his fingers into her rear entrance until his palm lay flush with the chastity belt.

The water rippled softly about them, the fragrance of evergreens and herbs perfuming the air, mingling with the musk of her arousal. Her high-pitched, breathy little cries when he splayed his fingers inside her tight rear passage urged him on. His cock throbbed harder. God's blood, how he needed to fuck her. To bury himself deep in her lush body, between her full red lips...within the tight, throbbing confines of her ass.

As he drew her pierced love button deeper in his mouth, twisting its ring with his tongue, Will envied the gold that kept her sopping cunt inviolate. Her juices flooded his hand when he worked a third finger up her ass and began to thrust slowly in and out. Her moans told him she was close...as close as he to losing control, finding the pleasure they both sought.

He nipped her clit then let it go and withdrew his fingers. "Turn around and kneel in the water. I want to fuck your pretty ass." He came up on his knees, guided himself to her well-lubricated rear entrance and grasped her hips. "Be not afraid, sweeting. I'll go slowly, and you'll love it. You're wet. So wet. Have you ever taken a man's cock like this?"

She trembled but leaned back, letting his cockhead press hard against her puckered opening. "Nay. But do not stop."

When he pressed a bit harder, her flesh unfurled like a flower in spring, allowing his cockhead past the tight ring of muscle before contracting, squeezing him almost painfully as her body tried to expel him. The water lapped at his thighs and ass, its warmth surrounding his shaft, caressing her bare ass, wetting the gold belt about her rounded ass cheeks and making it glitter in the candlelight.

God's teeth, 'twould be a miracle if he held out for long. His seed boiled up in his balls, threatened to erupt as he lowered her slowly, steadily, until her incredibly tight ass was fully impaled on his throbbing shaft. Her moans, louder now, bespoke pleasure—and pain. Pain he had no desire to exacerbate by moving.

It took all his control to be still. Not to thrust and withdraw hard and fast until he exploded in a fiery climax.

To keep from reaching around her and fondling her pretty, round breasts, rolling the nipples between his fingers. He resisted nipping her slender neck with his teeth, instead bathing her nape with his tongue, soothing motions to make her forget the pain and renew her arousal. Her skin warmed, and her little whimpers intensified. God in heaven, he'd never before aroused a woman quite so easily.

Her nipples stabbed at his palms when he cupped her breasts. Her tight ass gripped his cock almost painfully. The ungiving warmth of gold pressing on his seed sac reminded him of what he could not have, making him want even more to invade that sweet hole, fill it with his essence.

"Oh my lord. I ache."

"No more than I, my Meggie." Will lifted her slightly then lowered her again. He tried to concentrate not on the incredibly tight channel that gripped his cock but on the sensation of the wet, warm bath water sloshing over his thighs with every gentle motion he made. Her moans dissolved into breathy whimpers, and her nipples hardened further when he plucked them gently between his thumbs and forefingers.

Pressure built in his balls, made them tighten and throb more as her ass contracted around him and her whimpers became entreaties for him to fuck her, relieve the need she could no longer ignore. In answer, he lifted her higher, brought her down hard on his throbbing shaft. Again and again, until she resisted his effort to withdraw and clamped down on his cock.

"Oh yesss. More, my lord. Oh God."

Her screams of satisfaction sent him over the edge, and he joined her with a shout of his own as hot semen erupted from his body in hard, fast bursts.

"My lord?" she asked sleepily a few minutes later. "Does it feel this good with any man, or is it that what we just shared was special—that shining, breathtaking feeling the bards say come only between one man, one woman?"

"'Tis special, Meggie. Very special." For the first time in his twenty-one years, Will felt as though he might mean the reply he'd given countless lovers as a sop to their woman's need to make something special of an act that was as natural as breathing.

Chapter Six

Evelyn surveyed the bountiful feast laid before them at the high table but doubted she could eat a bite. Would that she'd not been so impulsive. If she had resisted the urge to learn if Gavin would desire her, she and her betrothed might be laughing and teasing each other now, instead of sitting silently now. As it was, she worried that any minute he might lash out at her again as he had many times since discovering her unwise deception.

Gavin's twin seemed besotted over the Scots lass. The two seemed unable to keep their hands off each other. Now Will leaned over and spoke to Gavin. What did he say?

Again Evelyn's cheeks grew hot. Mayhaps she could distract Gavin ere he could remind her again of her transgressions. "My lord, I'd give you a token this day, the first of the Christmas season."

Frowning, Gavin turned to her, took the small gold key she handed him. "'Tis a partridge etched upon a pear. Clever. I thank you, Madame." He dropped it into the pocket of the black velvet tunic he wore—a rich garment with the deVere device embroidered in brilliant tones of gold, red and purple.

"Do you not wish to know what it opens?" Evelyn asked.

"I'm certain you will enlighten me when it suits your purposes. Here. Eat some of the swan. I've never liked it." He paused, stared at her side of the silver plate they shared. "You've eaten hardly a bite."

"I'm not hungry." How could she have been, when it was so evident she inspired naught but disgust in the man who last night had practically drooled over her when he'd thought her one of the castle's whores. "Fret not. I'll not waste away from missing one or two meals."

"I mind not that you've got healthy curves. Besides, I'd not have you sicken. For better or worse, you'll be my wife. I'd have you healthy enough to bear my sons. Eat." Because his tone did not invite disobedience, Evelyn picked up a leg of swan. The savory treat might as well have been stale bread for all the enjoyment she took from eating it.

Later, while the Summerfield villeins trekked into the castle in small groups to pay their rents, partaking of mince pies and leftovers from the Christmas feast, Gavin directed the guests to sing, dance and generally make a mockery of civilized rules of behavior. Evelyn loved it. He might hate her, but he had a rather large cock and an obvious appetite for humor as well as fucking. Fortunately the merrymaking seemed to have taken the edge off his fury with her, or at least given him something more pleasant to do than ruminate about it.

After Will whispered something to Gavin, Gavin turned to her. "On the morrow we will join the Boxing Day hunt. Lady Margaret and Will wish to join us for another round of carnal play. Do not think of demurring."

Evelyn's cunt lips clenched, and her juices began to flow. "My lord—"

"Save the protests, Madame. You've proven well that you like your lovers in pairs. Be in the hall to break the fast, prepared to ride." He turned but looked back at her when she laid a hand on his thigh. "Yes?"

If he wanted to humiliate her, he apparently had found just the way to do it. The thought of parading naked before the lords and ladies of the castle made Evelyn cringe.

"Please, do not say we are to fuck outside, where any member of the hunting party might ride by and see? My lord, if you care not for me, give a care to what will be said of you."

Gavin laughed. "While I've fucked whores against handy trees, that's hardly what my lord brother and I have in mind for you. 'Tis too cold to disrobe out of doors, so we will use a hunting lodge secreted deep within the woods. I'd not have all know I'm taking a whore to wife. Go on now. The ladies have long since retired to their beds, 'tis time you do the same."

She'd been summarily dismissed, but she didn't mind. On the morrow Evelyn would turn the tables on her arrogant future husband who saw no problem in his constant debauchery while he roundly condemned her for the only slip in her own ladylike behavior — the only one he knew about, in any case.

* * * * *

The morn of Boxing Day broke clear and cold. Perfect for a hunt. Evelyn drew her deep-blue cloak around herself when a blast of frigid wind swept through the bailey, but her nether parts were warm, already damp with anticipation. Gavin might be intending to humiliate her by forcing her to re-enact her performance as Evie, but truth be known, the idea aroused her. She supposed she should be scandalized at the way her nipples puckered and her quim twitched for her handsome betrothed and his identical brother. Mayhaps she was as he said, the veriest of whores disguised in a lady's raiment.

She watched from her vantage point on the stair to the great hall as Lord William dragged Margaret of Clan MacFarlane up before him in the saddle. Looking at the assembled horseflesh, she singled out the great black destrier as Gavin's. Her own chestnut palfrey was nowhere to be found. Oh no. Surely he did not intend to toss her up with him as his brother had the Scots wench.

"Good morning, Evie," Gavin whispered when he came up behind her and lowered her cape. His breath felt warm on her earlobe, exposed now to the chilly wind. "Do you not think it strange that a peasant wench would mount her own fine steed?"

"I-I suppose."

His big hands grasped her at the waist. "You will ride with me. As my whore would do."

Evelyn held her breath when he lifted her, but he tossed her up onto the back of his horse as though she weighed no more than a babe. Only the way his muscles bunched beneath his fingers hinted at the slightest strain. When he mounted behind her, his rock-hard cock throbbed against the crack of her ass.

"We go first. They will follow." Gavin then lifted his hand, and the herald blew his horn. The hunt had begun.

Gavin wore no armor, only a leather gambeson Evelyn felt beneath the soft velvet of his tunic. When she leaned against his chest, the fabric caressed her cheek. And the bulk of his muscular body shielded her back from the wind. Her bottom ached from the enthusiastic loveplay during her role as Evie. It wasn't an unpleasant feeling. More an arousing one.

Her sire, were he alive, would not approve of the heat that bubbled in her belly or the strange light feeling she got in her belly when she looked upon her betrothed husband. She wished she knew whether he wanted her to be as wanton as she'd been as Evie, or if she should somehow demonstrate her loyalty by appearing uninterested in the sex play. Was he playing with her mind, enjoying her discomfort? What if she misread his signals, played the lady when he expected the whore? Worse, what if she thought he wanted a wanton wench when he expected a highborn lady?

Evelyn settled back against his massive chest, praying she'd make the right decision. Gavin led the party from the bailey then dropped back to ride beside Will and the Scots lass once they'd clattered over the massive wooden drawbridge.

The wind chilled her, but Gavin warmed her with his body heat. Evelyn held tight when he spurred his mount and distanced them from the crowd. "Were it not so cold, my wanton bitch, I'd be fucking you now. 'Tis good, rocking in a woman while my warhorse rocks me."

"Surely you jest." Gavin certainly would not fuck her before an audience of all in Lord Rolfe's court. In front of his lady mother. Or would he? From the way he fondled her mound through her gown, Evelyn was none too sure.

"Nay. I could put my cock in your sweet cunt and none would know but you…unless the pleasure was so great it would make you cry out for more. I warrant I can make you beg for it."

Just then three staccato notes burst out from somewhere behind them. "Evie."

Gavin's deep voice poured over her like honey. Yes, she liked him calling her that, even though he did it to humiliate her, remind her of her sin. "Mmmm?"

"The huntsman has cornered a boar. Wish you to be in on the kill, or shall we rest awhile in yonder hunting lodge?"

Evelyn shuddered at the thought of witnessing the gory battle between man and beast. And she sensed he wanted her to opt for him and sex. Briefly she considered saying she wished to watch the kill, but she wanted to please him more. "I want to be with you."

He pinched her nipple through the layers of her clothes then bent and whispered in her ear. "And Will. Don't forget Will. The one whose cock you took up the ass."

"Are you comfortable sharing your wife with your brother?

"As we shared our mother's womb, we share everything."

"Everything, m'lord?"

"Everything. And you like having two mouths, four hands on your body, caressing all your secret places. Two almost identical hard, randy cocks heating you, reaming your pretty mouth, cunt and ass, bringing you to pleasure beyond any you've known before."

'Twas wicked. Deliciously wicked. Evelyn's cream flowed, drenching her slit and dampening her quivering thighs as Gavin guided their mount to the secluded lodge. "That it provided pleasure does not make what we did less wrong. In truth, I find it hard to imagine greater joy than you gave me before." Difficult but not impossible. "How will I tell you and your brother apart? I swear, when I saw you both this morn I had no idea which one was you. Even though I've fucked with both of you," she added before he could remind her of that shameful fact.

"I guess you didn't see us together, did you?" He laughed. "'Tis said it's impossible to distinguish us but by the piercings of our cocks, though I am a bit taller...and some of our lovers have noted, a mite larger in the ballocks. You'll see the differences soon enough. I can tell by the sweet musk of sex that surrounds you that the idea of taking us both excites you."

Yes, it did, though Evelyn figured on rotting in hell for her wanton ways. Her nipples prickled in the morning chill when Gavin lifted her down from the saddle.

"Come, we'll not wait for my brother. I'm hot to fuck you now."

* * * * *

"Quiet. 'Twould seem Gavin's not alone." In truth Will was glad, for though he'd suggested the foursome to take his brother's mind off Lady Evelyn's deception, he was loath to share Meggie even with his twin. He also wondered at Gavin's uncharacteristic ire, wondered if he might have been stung by the same jealousy that now had him considering ways to keep Meggie to himself. "Come, let us not make our presence known. I'd introduce you to the pleasure of watching...seeing others find their pleasure."

"His cock looks more than ready, m'lord. Is yours?" Boldly Meggie reached inside Will's chausses, grasped his hardening shaft. "Oh yes. 'Tis wakening in my hand."

God's truth, the wench would kill him if she didn't stop rubbing her finger over his slit as she slowly rotated the thick gold bar that pierced his cockhead. "Cease, my sweet Meggie. I'd have you watch my twin and the buxom wench who sucks his cock so sweetly." He delved beneath her skirt and tugged gently at the ring in her clit.

"She strokes his ballocks. Look." Meggie sounded excited as she described what she saw.

"He likes it. Watch. His eyelids close. See how the sweat beads on his brow. I can practically feel him gasping for breath, fighting to hold in his seed. Watch. The wench torments him further."

Meggie gasped. "She put her finger up his bum, as ye did with me last night."

"It brings him pleasure. See. His cheeks flush. He can no longer stay still. Watch. He pulls away." Will pinched her clit between his thumb and forefinger, and her honey gushed around the shield that imprisoned her cunt. "Like that, don't you?"

"Oh yessss."

"Would you like to suck my cock?"

"Here?"

"Gavin would not mind."

She squeezed his balls, shot him a saucy grin. "Did I suck yer cock, m'lord, I'd not be able to watch your brother fuck his wench."

"All right. I'll suck your pretty clit then, whilst you tell me all Gavin does to the fair Evie."

"Evie? Lady Evelyn? It sounds as though ye know her well."

Did Will not know better, he'd have said Meggie'd been bitten by the green-eyed monster of jealousy. Or...mayhaps she had. "Intimately." Lowering his voice to a deep, soft rumble, he added, "Very, very intimately indeed. My brother and I made a fucking sandwich of her yestereve, ere I sent for you."

"M'lord?"

He nuzzled her smooth mound with his nose then met her gaze. "We fucked her the way I thought we'd do this day with you, sweeting. Me in her ass, Gavin in her mouth...and her tight, wet cunt. She's not trussed up the way you are. I can tell imagining us fucking you in tandem makes you wet. Hot." He stroked her clit, exerting pressure on the shield with its built-in dildo. "I'd taste your sweet honey now."

Will's tongue snaked out, flailed her ringed clit. "Tell me, Meggie. What does my brother do now?" he asked, the vibration tickling her clit and making her strain to thrust her flesh back into his mouth.

"He digs his fingers into the blond wench's hair and draws her face to his. Oooh. Do not stop, m'lord. Now he takes her mouth with his own, as though he's starvin' to taste himself on her reddened lips." She gasped as her cunt clenched, whimpering a little when Will pressed harder on her love button. "Yesss. That feels...so good. Makes me hot. Ye've got a magic touch."

He pulled away and blew on her swollen slit, sending shards of sensation down her quivering thighs. "Surely he doesn't stop there. If he does mayhaps he needs my help."

"He needs nothing, I swear. Evie straddles Gavin now. She's taking his big, beautiful ringed cock and stuffin' it in her cunt. She moans and whimpers as though she's in delicious pain as she sinks on his shaft clear up to his balls. My God, the jewels in his ballocks are winking at us now from between her splayed thighs. His smooth pink ball sac glistens with her juices."

"You like looking at my brother's balls? They'll be tickling your asshole soon enough." Reaching up, Will tweaked Meggie's nipples, making her gasp with delight and longing. "Go on. Surely they've not gone to sleep."

"Nay. He moves on her, harder and faster. Now he raises his body off her, cups her plump pale breasts. Oh yesss, my lord. Do not stop." She paused, breathing hard as delicious sensations flowed through her aching body. "Now he takes them in his mouth. First one, then the other of her dark, distended nipples disappear between his lips. His cheeks draw inward as he sucks upon them."

What delight the wench must be experiencing. Meggie tried to imagine the pleasure she'd feel if she had Will's huge, hard cock in her cunt and his soft, voracious mouth upon her less generous breasts.

Her nipples tingled. Her clit felt as though thousands of tiny needles danced within its tight confines and collided with the warm metal of the ring that held it. Her asshole twitched, as though telling her it was ready to take what was forbidden to her dripping cunt.

"Fuck me, m'lord. Rip away this cruel belt and put yer huge, hard cock inside me. I want what Sir Gavin's lover now so obviously enjoys."

Will raised his head but stroked Meggie's swollen slit with both his calloused hands. "I'd not hurt you. Do you want it, I will summon the armorer and have him free you. If he does, though, you must pay me a forfeit."

"Anything."

"Wed with me. Wed with me knowing I intend to destroy Clan MacFarlane, make its lands my own. Give the rotting castle you call home to my brother, that he may have holdings within a day's ride...that we may share you and share his bride as we've shared all since we were babes."

Will knew the price he asked was high. He realized full well that Meggie had likely been sent to spy on Summerfield. Still his blood boiled for the hot-blooded Scots lass. Nothing kept him from making a match for himself now that his betrothed had died of a fever nearly a year ago. "What say you? Would you be my English baroness now, and someday my countess, pray God that time comes not for many years?"

"You would slay my sire?"

"Not apurpose. I'd chase him back to the highlands from whence he came."

Meggie looked up at Will. "I canna ask more than that of ye, m'lord. Yes, if I be what you want, I'll be yer bride."

"Good. I'll order our priest to waive the banns, and we can wed and share the bridal bed with Gavin and his heiress. 'Tis what we've planned for all our lives—two compliant wenches to fuck us, together as well as separately."

"God forgive me for it's a heinous sin, but the thought of having ye both take me makes me hot and wet. I want ye so much it scares me."

"When we return to the castle, I will find the armorer." Will knelt at Meggie's feet and ran a finger under the shield of the gold belt. Carefully, he slipped it inside her dripping cunt beside the tongue-like plug. "He will remove this. 'Twill be your gift of gold to me this holiday season. Do you wish it, you may reinsert the ring and he can weld it shut. I wager it gives you great pleasure."

"Yes. As I imagine your jewels bring you joy." She stroked the length of his rod, tugging gently at each paired stud, grasping the jeweled ends of the thick bar and rotating them. Shards of intense pleasure began where metal touched flesh and spread cell by cell throughout his body. Lubrication pooled in the slit in his cockhead when she played with his balls. "Why do ye remove yer body hair?"

"To enhance my pleasure. Why do you remove yours?"

"To keep it from tangling in the iron maiden, or so thought my nursemaid when Da presented her with the device. I am sorry—"

"Do not be. I wish you always to keep your sweet slit smooth for me. Come, sit on my lap. I'd bring you to a climax for the last time ere I show you the ultimate woman's pleasure. Lift your gown, that I may fondle your pretty breasts whilst I bury my cock in your tight, hot ass."

Will wet his hand with Meggie's hot, slick cream then rubbed it over his cock. Positioning himself, he let her down inch by inch. Incredible tightness. Heat. Her rear entrance grabbed him, milked him, sucked him in until his balls rested against the puckered rosebud of her ass. When he reached under her gown and tugged on the hard nubs of her nipples, her breathy little whimpers nearly made him come.

His gaze locked with his brother's as Evie bobbed up and down on Gavin's cock. Gavin smiled. "A sandwich with two layers, my brother?" Will asked Gavin, and Meggie gave a breathy little laugh. "Plow her well, for in but three more days you'll take her for your bride."

Evie let out a scream, and Will watched Gavin's eyelids close. The look of ecstasy on his face, and the jerking movements of her buxom body above his twin, had Will ready to burst within Meggie's tight rear. As ready to burst as he sensed that she was.

Her heart beat fast and hard beneath his fingers. She clamped down on his cock with strong inner muscles, as if she'd never let him go. Her whimpers gave way to breathy moans of impending satisfaction, and her body trembled. Her slick wet honey drenched his balls and his thighs when he rocked beneath her and buried his cock to the hilt. Her climax sent him over the edge, and he felt his seed building then spilling, scalding his cock within the tight confines of her rear passage.

* * * * *

His lust sated, Gavin was feeling mellow toward his wanton betrothed. He could have as easily been stuck with a withered prune of a woman. Instead, he was about to gain a wife he loved to fuck. One it would be a pleasure to get his heirs on.

Still naked, he lay back on the cushions by the fireplace in the hunting lodge and watched Evie gather her garments that he'd strewn about in his haste to get to her pale, generous flesh. He liked her alabaster skin, the full curves of her breasts and buttocks, the roundness of her belly that cushioned him, keeping her hipbones from digging into his flesh the way skinny women's did.

Her smile warmed him, whether they were fucking or sitting at the high table before his family and their retainers. The demeanor the jongleur had seen as haughty, Gavin read as the mark of a strong chatelaine who'd keep his castle folk in line, thus keeping him comfortable and well-fed. Evie didn't hesitate to speak her mind, but she did so with good humor and consideration for those who served her.

And by God's bones he loved burying his cock in her soft, tight cunt. Loved pleasuring her and taking pleasure in her. That alone made him content with his bride. He raked her with an approving gaze, glad she apparently had no worries about him seeing her as God had made her. Gavin liked that too. The only thing he didn't like was the thought of sharing her with men other than Will.

'Twouldn't happen. He'd keep her so stuffed with his cock that she'd be too weary to even think of straying. And if he had to go away, he could always confine her in one of the castle's three towers.

All in all, Gavin was content. He could have done worse. Much worse. Instead he'd been given a wanton bride who made his blood boil, and rich lands to rule. Returning Evelyn's smile, he reached for his own clothes and started to dress. Suddenly he was anxious to get on with the revelry of the season—and the celebration of his wedding.

Will's too, he'd wager from the protective way his brother had treated the MacFarlane lass. Two hot-blooded brides for the brothers to share—though for the first time in his life, Gavin was feeling a hint of need to keep this one woman for himself alone.

He shrugged off that emotion as a result of the afterglow of a good fucking—no, a great one, the best he could recall ever having enjoyed. 'Twas the enthusiastic whore in her that he lusted after, but he found he was also coming to like the fine widow lady who was to become his bride. "Come, my hot, sweet wanton, we must return to Summerfield and resume our roles as prospective bride and groom, ere we are missed."

Chapter Seven

Later that afternoon the Yule log crackled in the fire, its sap perfuming the air with a clean, woodsy scent. The serfs came in groups, and straggling one by one, to claim their gifts from the earl and countess. Giggling maidservants hung fresh garlands of mistletoe about the hall, while the older housemaids served honey cakes and the earl's finest wine to the family and their guests. After they sat to partake of the evening meal, Lord Rolfe lifted his glass and proposed a toast.

"To my heir, Sir William, and the woman he's chosen for his own. May they have the joy I've found with my Jasmine...the prosperity God has granted Summerfield...a long life together and many sturdy sons."

Gavin lifted his cup to toast his brother, genuinely happy that Will had made a love match. He glanced at his own betrothed, full of pride in her with her fine garb and pretty manners, yet sad in a way that he'd fallen in love not with her but with the bawdy castle whore she'd portrayed—the Evie he couldn't acknowledge in noble company—Lord of Misrule or not.

Evelyn spoke cordially with his lady mother about some boring household crisis while all Gavin wanted to do was lift her skirts, put her on his lap and fuck her until she screamed. Mayhaps he'd do that once they wed—and once they went to live on her property a day's ride distant.

Gavin fingered the gift she'd bestowed on him this night—a matched pair of turtle doves beautifully crafted of gold, their beaks hinged and poised to clamp down upon his nipples—or hers. The two were joined by a finely wrought chain. "I'd try these on your tits tonight," he whispered once the carolers began to sing.

"They're for you, not me. Would you like for me to—"

"No." He had the feeling the bite on his nipples would flow straight to his cock, and he'd be hard as stone and hurting ere he could possibly retire for the night. With her. Strangely, neither Mavis nor any of the other wenches he'd bedded held much appeal compared with his buxom Evie. Evelyn. His betrothed.

* * * * *

Two days hence, Gavin tossed Will the latest gift. Evelyn's maid had delivered it moments earlier—a cleverly made cock cage bearing four golden bands, each etched with a calling bird upon a perch. The pear-shaped partridge key she'd given him on Christmas Day fit easily into the tiny lock on the device. As with the nipple clips, the cage was a fine piece of goldsmithing.

Damn, he'd thought the series of provocative toys had been broken yestereve when Evelyn had served him three plump roasted guinea hens for their evening meal.

"Tomorrow 'twill be five gold rings she gives you," Will commented while making a show of examining the cage and the heavy gold chains that would lock it to the wearer's body. "Pray God the rings do not fit through *this*."

"True."

Will looked again at the golden cage, laughed. "Mayhap she intends to fuck with me whilst you watch. Or…"

That would happen over Gavin's dead body. He'd share, but he wouldn't sit idly and watch another man fuck Evie, even if it was his twin brother. "Begone with you. Go to the armorer and have him cut away the iron maiden that keeps you from your lady's cunt. Then you will have something to occupy yourself other than tormenting me."

* * * * *

The fifth day of Christmas. A holy day of celebration for all, what should have been a joyous day at Summerfield. A feast fit for King Henry himself. Gavin lounged at the high table, a jeweled coronet perched precariously upon his head, a joint of venison held high like a scepter in one large, powerful hand.

Evelyn smiled at her handsome raven-haired bridegroom, glancing past him to his identical twin and the MacFarlane lass, now Lord William's bride. The Yule log crackled cheerily in the huge fireplace, warding off the chill from a cold, damp wind that howled beyond the castle walls. The air of gaiety that prevailed in the hall didn't extend to her, for her husband's last order had cast a pall on her enjoyment of the wedding festivities.

Her cheeks still burned when she recalled his words moments earlier. "A joyous day indeed. Drink a toast to two brides for me and Will, one blond and buxom, the other slender with hair of flames. One bedding. 'Tis my order as Lord of Misrule. As we've shared all else, so my lord brother and I will share the women we've wed this night."

Lady Jasmine had gasped before consulting with Lord Rolfe and composing her beautiful face into a smile. The Summerfield knights and men-at-arms had let out with cheers and all manner of ribald comments. Meggie had blushed prettily and whispered something that made her husband grab her for a long, public kiss.

Gavin had merely raised his joint of venison and swigged another goblet of wine.

Jongleurs, ropedancers and minstrels vied for his approval, for as Lord of Misrule, his word was law. None dared to defy him, not even Evelyn, who despite her embarrassment looked forward to the public bedding that would come ere long.

"Wine, more wine for all!" Gavin's voice rang out over the sensual sounds of lutes and harps, sweet voices of the wandering minstrels.

"We await th' bedding, m'Lord of Misrule!" exclaimed Alex, Will's squire.

Gavin clapped his hands. "Then wait no more, my friends, for my cock is randy, my bride ripe for the plucking. I wager Will's as ready as I to sow his seed. Will?"

"To the bedchamber, ladies. We will soon follow." Gavin turned to Will after the women guests had dragged their brides away. "What did your fair lady gift you with this day?"

"A gift of gold. Her maidenhead, bared for the taking. For locking her in that wicked device, Laird MacFarlane deserves to die of apoplexy at the news that his one surviving bairn now belongs to his sworn enemy. With what did your bride present you?"

"As you predicted. Five gold rings." A signet ring bearing the fitzSimmons device, two identical rounded gold bands for his forefingers...and the fourth and fifth, smooth circular rings too wide for any of his fingers yet not wide enough to span his wrists. "The MacFarlane knows not of the marriage?" Gavin had watched a contingent of armed knights and men ride out the day before to carry the news of the upcoming nuptials about the countryside. He'd assumed the countryside included the rotting MacFarlane keep that lay a stone's throw across the contested border.

"'Nay. The party rode out yesterday to ensure peace for this day's festivities. The news of my marriage to Meggie I thought to impart personally, after we consummate our vows. Come, my brother, it is past time we did our husbandly duties."

Gavin drained the rest of his fine red Flemish wine. "Come. We must not keep our women waiting."

* * * * *

Meggie tossed back her flaming locks, met Evelyn's gaze. "What troubles ye, milady?"

"Only that it suits me not to be mounted like a prize mare for all to see." At the sound of heavy footsteps on the solar stair, Lady Evelyn struggled to arrange her hip-length blond locks. 'Twas a poor job they did, hiding her pale, plump form from view—but she had naught better, for the ladies who attended them had vanished with all their garments. She spared a glance at Meggie, who seemed not to care that her compact tits and ass were in plain view of all who might wish to see.

Despite the warmth of the fire, Evelyn trembled. Not from fear. God knew she'd done this before. She'd spread her legs for all to see and flushed with embarrassment when old Baron fitzSimmons had hoisted the bloody sheets and proclaimed his ownership of her person. Proclaimed his manhood for all to see. Ha. Manhood indeed. The rutting old bastard had cared naught for her pleasure, only his own. At least the new man her estates had bought her knew how to wield his jeweled cock. And gave every appearance of loving to wield it on her.

As did his identical twin, the Scotswoman's eager bridegroom. Evelyn would take part in this pagan ritual, the joining of two men, two women. Truth be known, she'd enjoy once again experiencing the twin lovers stuffing her every orifice, bringing her to pleasure.

What she'd not like one bit was watching her husband dipping his randy wick in his brother's young bride. 'Twould make her blood boil to see Gavin caressing Meggie while her own soft flesh craved his mouth, the touch of his calloused fingertips. Mayhaps...the cock cage should remain. He'd not fuck her, but then he couldn't fuck Meggie either. He could only arouse them with his tongue, his hands.

Nay, 'twould never do. Evelyn could never more forego the incredible fullness that came with having that cock stuffing her cunt, spurting its hot seed deep into her womb. 'Twas good Gavin held the key, for he'd certainly dispense with that gift without delay if indeed he'd chosen to honor her gift by wearing it ere they wed.

Evelyn glanced again at Lord William's bride, trying not to compare their bodies but failing miserably. Her husband had gained a plump widowed pigeon, two years his senior, while his twin possessed an auburn-haired beauty still fresh and ripe for picking. Knowing she'd bought her bridegroom with land and titles did little to quell the sense of inadequacy that gripped Evelyn. Nothing to squelch the growing reluctance to share her man with one so fair and lovely.

They came. 'Twas not the time for trembling like an untried girl, which she certainly was not. Instead she'd pour out her growing feelings for Gavin in her touch, her kisses. In her enthusiastic participation in the ritual that meant so much to him and Will. With a deliberately lascivious expression, Evelyn raked her husband's and his brother's naked bodies with undisguised interest.

Mirror images, each tall and strong, each bearing bride-gifts in identical casks clad in gold and set with precious stones, Gavin and Will stood before Evelyn and Meggie, as naked as when they left their mother's womb but for the winking jewels in their cocks. Laughing, jesting knights and men-at-arms shouted bawdy suggestions as they ogled the brides their lord's eldest sons had taken this day.

Gavin's cock stood at attention, the glittering ring in its head glowing in the candlelight, its magnificent shaft encased in the cage Evelyn had ordered fashioned to ensure his faithfulness. Jewels winked at her from the studs that passed through his corona. Will's cock sparkled too. He lacked the cage and the ring passing through his slit. Instead he had a jewel-crowned bar that entered the head of his swollen phallus on one side and emerged on the other. Accouterments Evelyn hadn't noted the other night when he'd introduced himself by kneeling at her back and plowing her ass with his big, hard sword.

Mmmm. Taking them both at once had given her a heady rush...a climax the likes of which she'd never known before. Still... Sir Gavin was her husband, bought and paid for. Share him with Will's bride? By God, only on her terms!

Evelyn dragged her gaze from Meggie's husband, settled it upon her own. "Like you what you see?" she asked him, taking care to look him in the eye. Hoping not to read longing for the fair Meggie there.

"Yes, wife. Sweep back the pale curtain that hides your bounty from my eyes. I'd see all of you. I'd have Will view your bounteous charms as well. 'Tis only fair, for I can plainly see his bride."

Vowing she'd not be stung by the inevitable comments some of the drunken guests would make about her girth, Evelyn did as Gavin bid, sweeping her pale locks over one shoulder, revealing her heaving breasts, her rounded belly and generous thighs. Her cunt creamed at the thought of once again becoming the filling in a sandwich fuck, taking two hard bodies, two rigid cocks pounding her ass, her cunt.

She wanted them both and yet…having them would mean she'd have to watch whilst Gavin joined Will in fucking the Scots maid.

Nay. She'd wed with Gavin. She'd have him to herself. His hungry eyes swept over her, swept the expected catcalls and insults from her mind. 'Twas no doubt about it. For all that her lord husband might chide her for having deceived him, he found her desirable. Even now his caged cock stood in salute not for his brother's beautiful bride but for her.

Meggie looked at Evelyn then shifted her gaze back to Will. Sweeping back her titian curls, she stood proudly, smoothly naked before his appreciative eyes. "Come, if ye see no flaws in me. I'd have ye consummate this marriage, fill the aching empty sheath between my thighs. I'd have ye first ere ye share me wi' yer bonny brother."

"I too would have my husband's fine cock all to myself ere we share." Evelyn reached out and caught Gavin's cock ring with one finger. "I see you chose to wear my gift. I like it."

Gavin glanced down at his trussed-up flesh and grimaced. "I do not, my lady." He tossed her the golden key. "I order you to remove it so we may get on with the business of fulfilling the vows we've made. As your husband, Madame, notwithstanding the fact I'm also Lord of Misrule."

Evelyn watched Will scoop Meggie easily up in his arms and toss her on the huge marriage bed. When they began to fuck, she averted her gaze. The men crowded in the solar doorway cheered. Evelyn hated it—the ritual bedding, the splitting asunder of a virgin bride by her husband while a drunken horde of his men watched and shouted ribald suggestions.

Fuckfests were well and good when all participated. Not when some watched and shouted obscenities at the participants. "Send the observers away, husband, and I will remove it. Then we may get on with the bedding. I'm no virgin whose blood need be attested to."

Gavin stepped closer, cupped her chin in his hand. The smile he bestowed on her surrounded her with warmth, like a velvet robe. "But I am a man whose cock has been caged by his lady. I'd have witnesses to its removal."

Agreeing that made sense, she knelt and fumbled with the tiny lock. For a moment Meggie's little cry distracted Evelyn, but she persevered. The crowd's cheer resounded in her ears when she knelt and unlocked the cage from Gavin's cock and balls. When she slid it off, she saw he'd discovered the use for the two largest rings she'd gifted him with today. The largest ringed his cock and ballocks, while the smaller encircled the base of his huge, swollen cock.

"I stand ready to bring you pleasure, my lady wife," he told her as a cheer went up from the assembled men. "Watch…"

Gavin raised Evelyn to her feet then lifted her in his arms. He strained a bit but steadied himself quickly and strode with her to the marriage bed. "Spread your legs, madame, that I may fuck you for our guests' pleasure. Then I will order them away and the fuckfest may begin."

Evelyn's cream flowed heavy despite her embarrassment at the prospect of taking her husband's huge ringed cock before the drunken wedding guests. When Gavin knelt between her legs and sank slowly into her cunt, he looked her in the eye.

"All right, my friends. The Lady Evelyn is mine in deed as well as words, as is Lady Margaret now my brother's true wife. As Lord of Misrule, I order you all to seek your own beds. Prepare for more festivities on the morrow!" Gavin's voice rang out, his authority unquestionable.

"Thank you, my lord."

"You are welcome. I'd not cause you discomfort, but our guests demanded that they be allowed to bear witness to our joining." Bracing his upper body on his elbows, he bent and brushed her lips with his own. "They are leaving now. And they'll not return."

Evelyn brushed a lock of dark hair off her husband's forehead. "I beg your forgiveness for my deception, Gavin. I'd not have it cast a pall on our marriage."

"'Tis all right, sweeting. 'Tis my pleasure to have found a bride who takes pleasure in the marriage bed. One who keeps my cock stiff and ready any time she's near." He laid his head on Evelyn's breast and drew a nipple into his mouth.

As he rocked in and out of her dripping cunt, she grew hotter and wetter with each stroke. "Oh yesss. Fuck me harder. Please."

Her clit tingled every time Gavin ground his hips and brushed it with the rigid base of his cock. God's blood, but having him fuck her like this — as though his whole mind centered on her — made her every reaction more intense. Hotter.

Vaguely her mind registered that Will was also moving on Meggie, his rhythm in perfect harmony with Gavin's. Meggie's little whimpers triggered her own ecstatic moans as the pressure built in her cunt, began spreading...bursting...blinding her with its intensity. Oh God in heaven, she was dying. Scalding waves of the most intense pleasure she'd ever known washed over her, made her gasp for breath.

Was that her scream? Or Meggie's? Evelyn was past thinking. Past anything but savoring the exquisite pleasure that flowed from Gavin's pulsating cock in her cunt, consumed her in a burst of delicious sensations. His shout and the hard bursts of his seed into her womb set off yet another wave of intense pleasure.

* * * * *

As the sun rose, illuminating the tower room he'd shared with Will since they left the nursery, Gavin lay between his wife and Will's. His cock throbbed in Meggie's mouth while he feasted on Evelyn's creamy cunt. The ruby-glass plug in her ass shone in the sunlight. At this moment he couldn't figure why he'd been so angry at her deception. Why it had taken so long for him to realize what a jewel he now possessed.

God's nightshirt, but he'd been given a prize. Ripe and buxom and hot-blooded as hell. Not to mention that she'd elevated him from knight to lord with the saying of their vows. On top of that, Gavin liked his bride. Enjoyed being with her outside their bedchamber as well as in it. Yes, he was one lucky man. Wanting to hear her scream with pleasure, he sucked her swollen clit between his teeth and flailed it with his tongue. Will had her mouth, tongue-fucking it the way he'd tongue-fucked Meggie's earlier.

Now Meggie sucked his cock, tangling her tongue in the ring when she licked the drops of lubrication from it. The way she clutched his ass cheeks, digging in with her nails while Evelyn held onto his waist, drove him wild. When Will plowed Meggie's cunt, she moved her mouth in that same rhythm on Gavin's cock.

Gavin plunged his tongue deep into Evelyn's cunt, savored her cream. His balls tightened as Meggie sucked him harder, deeper.

"My God, Meggie. I'm cominggg!" Will shouted.

Meggie clamped down on Gavin's cock, her whimpers reverberating on his distended flesh. He gasped at the delicious sensation, half withdrew the dildo from Evelyn's sweet ass and plunged it back in, hard, while he latched onto her clit with his mouth and sucked hard.

The first waves of his climax shook him. Shook them. Hot, hard jets of semen bounced off Meggie's throat, making her swallow. That motion triggered more spasms, more come. As Meggie swallowed the last of his come, Evelyn screamed out her pleasure. And Will collapsed onto Meggie, pressing her skinny body into Gavin's while he wrapped his arms about his wife's quaking thighs.

"Damn it, Will, roll over. Hold your wife and let me hold mine."

* * * * *

"'Twill be the last time we all four share each other, I vow," Gavin told Evelyn later as she lay with him after Will and Meggie had left the room.

"Why, my lord husband? I find sharing exhilarating."

"Because I'd honor my vows?" The smile he gave her nearly took her breath away. "Nay. 'Tis that I'm greedy. I'd have my beautiful, buxom bride all to myself. Think one man can see to all your carnal needs, love?"

He called her "love". Did he mean it? Dared she admit she loved him too? "We shall see, husband. May I assume you've truly forgiven me for my little deception on Christmas Eve?"

"I forgave you days ago." He looked at her, merriment and mischief showing in his dark eyes, his quirky grin. "I think, though, you need a lesson so you won't try to deceive me again. Rise. Fetch yon riding whip from atop my trunk. I'll punish you now, and the deed will be hence forgotten."

Her milky ass cheeks felt soft as silk to Gavin as he positioned her across his thighs to take her punishment. "So pretty. So soft. Pity to turn them red and sore." Reluctantly, for he hated to hurt his love, he raised and lowered the crop once…twice…three times. Welts stared up at him, made him cringe at the thought he was hurting her.

"More. Punish me more, my lord."

He hit her again, harder this time. She yelped but begged him to continue. Shifting the crop to his other hand, he reached between her legs, felt her honey flowing. "Mayhaps I'll use this in our loveplay since you like it so well."

"Oh yesss. Please fuck me now. Fuck me hard and well."

Slowly he slid her onto the bed, face up, sliding between her thighs and looping her legs over his shoulders. "With pleasure. And with love. Open to me, wife, I'd fill you with my seed."

Evelyn sighed. "And with love. Always with love."

After she came, after she'd wrung the last drop of seed from his exhausted cock, Evelyn rolled onto her side and cupped his face between her soft hands. "I love you too, my husband. Forever."

Epilogue
Summerfield Castle, Christmastide 1179

ഌ

'Twas Christmas Eve, a time for prayer and celebration—and revelry about to be presided over by his third son Henry, just knighted by his uncle ere he came home for the holiday. Earl Rolfe stretched his long legs before him, wondered if fourteen years hence he'd be having an iron maiden fit on Alisa, who now tugged on his knee, begging for a ride. Just yesterday he'd caught Henry and Alfred fucking with a willing serf girl in the hunting lodge their brothers used to use for some of their debauchery.

Rolfe stared into the flame, his mood reflective. Two years ago today he'd given Jasmine the daughter they'd wanted for years. Two years ago this blessed season, Gavin and Will had taken brides. And nearly two years ago, once the Epiphany had passed, they'd rid the northern marches of the scourge of Clan MacFarlane.

"Papa?"

"Yes, sweeting." Though he loved all his children, his little girl held a special place in his heart.

"Play wif' nef..."

"You want to play with your nephews? Ask your nanny to take you to them." Rolfe imagined his young namesake, just three months old, was partaking of nourishment from his mama's now-bounteous breasts, and that Gavin's twins would be wakening from their naps. "Run along now. I'd spend some time alone with your mama ere we go to the hall for the noontide meal."

"The season has her excited beyond all," he told Jasmine when she joined him on the settle before the fire. "Happy Christmas, my love."

"Yes. 'Tis happy indeed to have everyone home…and to know Gavin will be moving within an hour's ride once he rebuilds that rockpile Meggie's sire once called a castle."

Rolfe stroked Jasmine's thigh, as firm and slender now as it had been years ago when he took her as his leman and then his bride. "You cannot wait to have his twins nearby to spoil, as you spoil Will and Meggie's now. Admit it."

"All right. I do want them close to spoil them. But also so I may see how well the match you made for Gavin has turned out. It makes me happy to know it's not property but love that keeps a smile on my boy's face."

"'Tis strange. Motherhood has slimmed Evelyn while it's fattened Meggie." His cock twitching as he inhaled Jasmine's familiar scent, Rolfe slid his hand higher, caressed her slit through the layers of her shift and gown. "They change, whilst you bear my babes and stay as lovely as you were the day we met."

Turning into his embrace, Jasmine laughed. "Beauty is in the eyes of the beholder, love. It warms me to know you see me now as I was then—even though my reflection in the garden pool tells me otherwise. Come, let me show you how much I love you…how much I love how you love me."

Later, sated and content, Rolfe and Jasmine lay among the furs in their cozy bed. "Rolfe?"

"Yes, sweeting." He turned his head, met her sapphire gaze.

"I wonder if our twin sons still share each other's wives."

"What?" He'd explained their wedding night away as a one-time ritual understandable for brothers who'd shared their mother's womb.

"I've known since they weren't much older than Henry is now." She ran a teasing finger down his chest, stopping to tweak the rings in his nipples ere moving on to stroke his jeweled cock.

"That ended the day after their weddings, I believe. Like me, our sons seem content with the women they married."

"I suppose now all we must do is worry about Henry and Alfred," she said, cupping his balls and giving them a gentle squeeze.

Rolfe laughed. "I fear our worries about them will be naught compared with what we'll face with Alisa when the time comes. 'Tis no way she can be her parents' daughter and not give us a trial."

"Mayhaps you should marry her off ere she's out of nappies, then."

"Or mayhaps not. I welcome the challenge of keeping our daughter from the hands of lechers like our sons." He noticed Jasmine's grin, decided to say it before she could. "And like me."

"Thank God, like you. We'd best rise and see to our family and guests. Rolfe, I love you now as I've loved you for twenty-four long years."

"I too. I pray we'll have as many more."

Why an electronic book?

We live in the Information Age—an exciting time in the history of human civilization, in which technology rules supreme and continues to progress in leaps and bounds every minute of every day. For a multitude of reasons, more and more avid literary fans are opting to purchase e-books instead of paper books. The question from those not yet initiated into the world of electronic reading is simply: *Why?*

1. ***Price.*** An electronic title at Ellora's Cave Publishing and Cerridwen Press runs anywhere from 40% to 75% less than the cover price of the exact same title in paperback format. Why? Basic mathematics and cost. It is less expensive to publish an e-book (no paper and printing, no warehousing and shipping) than it is to publish a paperback, so the savings are passed along to the consumer.
2. ***Space.*** Running out of room in your house for your books? That is one worry you will never have with electronic books. For a low one-time cost, you can purchase a handheld device specifically designed for e-reading. Many e-readers have large, convenient screens for viewing. Better yet, hundreds of titles can be stored within your new library—on a single microchip. There are a variety of e-readers from different manufacturers. You can also read e-books on your PC or laptop computer. (Please note that Ellora's Cave does not endorse any specific brands.

You can check our websites at www.ellorascave.com or www.cerridwenpress.com for information we make available to new consumers.)

3. ***Mobility.*** Because your new e-library consists of only a microchip within a small, easily transportable e-reader, your entire cache of books can be taken with you wherever you go.

4. ***Personal Viewing Preferences.*** Are the words you are currently reading too small? Too large? Too… ANNOYING? Paperback books cannot be modified according to personal preferences, but e-books can.

5. ***Instant Gratification.*** Is it the middle of the night and all the bookstores near you are closed? Are you tired of waiting days, sometimes weeks, for bookstores to ship the novels you bought? Ellora's Cave Publishing sells instantaneous downloads twenty-four hours a day, seven days a week, every day of the year. Our webstore is never closed. Our e-book delivery system is 100% automated, meaning your order is filled as soon as you pay for it.

Those are a few of the top reasons why electronic books are replacing paperbacks for many avid readers.

As always, Ellora's Cave and Cerridwen Press welcome your questions and comments. We invite you to email us at Comments@ellorascave.com or write to us directly at Ellora's Cave Publishing Inc., 1056 Home Avenue, Akron, OH 44310-3502.

COMING TO A BOOKSTORE NEAR YOU!

ELLORA'S CAVE

Bestselling Authors Tour

UPDATES AVAILABLE AT
WWW.ELLORASCAVE.COM

Cerridwen, the Celtic Goddess of wisdom, was the muse who brought inspiration to storytellers and those in the creative arts. Cerridwen Press encompasses the best and most innovative stories in all genres of today's fiction. Visit our site and discover the newest titles by talented authors who still get inspired - much like the ancient storytellers did, once upon a time.

Cerridwen Press
www.cerridwenpress.com

Discover for yourself why readers can't get enough of the multiple award-winning publisher Ellora's Cave.

Whether you prefer e-books or paperbacks, be sure to visit EC on the web at www.ellorascave.com

for an erotic reading experience that will leave you breathless.